Short Christians

Exploring Faith Together
Through Fiction

Liz Jennings

'...Since we've compiled this long and sorry record as sinners
... and proved that we are utterly incapable
of living the glorious lives God wills for us,
God did it for us.
Out of sheer generosity he put us in right standing with himself.
A pure gift.
He got us out of the mess we're in and restored us
to where he always wanted us to be.
And he did it by means of Jesus Christ.'

Romans 3:23-24

"I am a practising Christian.
I have to keep practising,
coz I never can get it right."

Maya Angelou

DEDICATION

This book is dedicated to my dear Dad,
the Reverend Graham Hayles,
who passed away on November 11th, 2016.
I expect he would proclaim himself the shortest Christian of all,
but to me - and many others - with his gentle certainty and patient love,
his kind brown eyes and firm hand clasp,
he was and always will be
a true giant of the faith.

CONTENTS

ACKNOWLEDGEMENTS

Thank you...

Elsa and Claire from Lioness,
for your belief and encouragement from the word go.
James for your eagle-eyed proofreading and wise editorial feedback.
Mark, Maisie and Reuben for your support over many years of writing,
despairing, celebrating, despairing, writing, despairing etc. etc.
Isobel for your encouragement in epic doses.
Michelle for pushing me to keep trying,
and for introducing me to Elsa.
Mum, for always asking how it was going,
and listening to my angst and ramblings.
All the small groups and churches I've ever been a member of,
for teaching me so much about what it means to be part of God's family.
Carrie, Elizabeth, Melissa, Ruth and Sarah
for being such willing guinea pigs in the reading and discussing
of these stories: you'll never know how exciting it was
for me to hear your responses to them
– couldn't sleep for hours
after small group evenings!

INTRODUCTION

Short Christians contains twelve short stories, which follow the lives of Christian characters through a particular moment in their faith journeys. I hope you'll find it engaging and thought provoking.

I've always found that fiction gives me the best starting point for reflecting on life, and helps me to think things through in fresh ways. My hope is that this collection will enable you to do just that, thinking, reflecting and sharing ideas with others to find fresh points of connection in a relaxed, enjoyable and stimulating way.

Having tested the stories in my own small group, I've been amazed at the discussions they've led to, and thrilled by the easy way that they led us to deeper levels of honesty and engagement with each other.

While none of the characters depicted are based on real people, I hope you'll find that their stories contain truths within the fiction, and that you are able to relate to them in one way or another, and perhaps identify with some of their experiences.

To me, as a writer, all of these characters are 'real' - despite breathing only in my imagination. For each story I wrote, whether the characters were lovely or otherwise, I was very aware that, should they ever happen to exist in the real world, God would love them completely and utterly.

I heard a phrase once about people who do their job badly and yet, despite all the evidence proclaiming their lack of ability, get promoted anyway. The phrase was 'failing upwards.' It strikes me, writing this, that 'failing upwards' is the very thing we engage in as followers of Christ. Every day, we fail - and yet, by God's unending grace, he loves us and draws us ever closer to him.

This collection is a celebration of the grace and hope that we all have in Jesus, whoever we are, whatever we've done, however we're feeling, whatever we're going through.

If you are using this book within a small group setting, I hope that you'll find that your discussions are times of increased honesty, greater connection, deeper understanding and growing love for one another.

Liz Jennings
September 2017

GUIDELINES FOR LEADERS

How to use the stories

The first thing to do as a group is to agree on a story to read for the following week's session together. The stories can be read in any order you like, and with twelve, they could take you through a term quite easily. I've included a brief description for each story with the contents list and again at the beginning of that story's section, so you might like to use this information to guide you in your choice – or, alternatively, simply work your way through the stories in the order they appear.

Exploring a story's theme together

It will certainly be helpful in your group sessions to read with an awareness of the themes of each story. I've listed the themes I could see emerging in the 'Author Notes' section towards the back of the book, but you may find things I haven't seen there – that's the beauty of fiction; each person's approach will be unique.

At the beginning of each discussion time, it will be worth asking your group if they picked up on themes that I have not listed. It's easy to do – just ask everybody in your group to call out all the words they think of when they remember the story. These words will give you all the themes that people picked up on – they may be things like 'hypocrisy,' 'spin,' or 'pride,' or they may be voiced in different ways, e.g. someone might say 'She's scared of birds,' in which case you can identify from that the word 'fear.'

Discussion Times

I've tried to pose questions which should lead to useful discussion in response to each story, so if you use the discussion prompts, they will give you a clear structure to follow through.

However, don't be afraid to spend time over people's general initial response to a story. There's no rule about sticking to the questions I've raised, and you may have a much more beneficial and applicable discussion time as a result – so please, do feel free to go off-piste if the conversation is fruitful!

Using the Questions

After each story you'll find a set of questions under the heading 'Let's Talk'. These are designed to get your group discussing aspects and elements of the story in a quick and easy way. They will hopefully lead to lively, thought provoking, productive and enjoyable discussion together.

I've inserted spaces for readers to jot down their answers, as I found that this was the way my own small group instinctively used the printed-off stories I gave them. Please do encourage group members that they only need to share what they choose to share – they may write things which they prefer to keep for private reflection, and that must, of course, be respected.

Using the Quotes

The questions are followed by some quotes from The Message, under the heading 'Let's Listen', bringing God's voice into your discussion times in biblical form.

You may well be reminded of other Bible verses as you read, and it would be great to encourage each other to bring these into your group discussion times too, to shed further light on issues that arise through your reading of the stories.

Some of the verses may be challenging. Don't shy away from them, but use them to further your discussion and prayer; wrestle with them, question God about them – be honest in your responses to them.

Praying Together

Accompanying each story and discussion time are a couple of prompts under the heading 'Let's Pray', to help you to pray as a group at the end of your evening. They're short and sweet, and generally encourage you to pray around whatever issues the discussion has raised. If they don't fit the way your group prays, please don't feel bound by them. I've written them as if speaking to just one reader, but they will work for your group as well as for individuals.

As ever, sensitivity is required when praying in groups; some people will want to share, while others will not. Enforced sharing is terrifying for group members, and inappropriate in a setting where you're aiming to build one another up. At the same time, fostering a place where believers pursue intimacy and honesty before God will move us all on in our journeys of faith.

Spend time praying and listening for God's voice; seek out his heart of compassion and direction for your group.

Note down any thoughts that come from the group that could enhance and improve your prayer life together.

If you're not doing it already, you might like to try a time of regular silent listening with your group where you wait, eyes closed, in active anticipation of hearing from God. I began doing this a few years ago: I'm very much the beginner, and rarely manage more than a few minutes of listening – and yet these are the times when God has spoken to me most clearly – I suppose because I've finally stopped talking and given him the chance to say something!

I've practised this technique within a small group setting, too, and, although at first the silence made us all a bit self-conscious, it proved very fruitful and encouraging for each group member, wherever they were at in their own lives that week. I'd really recommend risking the social awkwardness of silence in order to hear from God!

Of course, there are as many ways of hearing from God as there are pray-ers. This is a great chance to chat and hear from each other about the unexpected ways God speaks to each of you.

At the end of each 'Let's Pray' section, I've included a brief space to write, so that readers can use this book as a prayer journal, too. Please ensure your group know that they will not be asked to share this prayer journal in group times, it is entirely personal and for their own private use.

The Importance of Confidentiality in Building Trust and Intimacy

As always, a key to group intimacy is to have a policy of 'what's said in small group, stays in small group,' and to respect that what comes out through discussion and in prayer is for the ears of this group at this time only (unless of course it's something that has legal ramifications, in which case take it to your church leadership and follow the appropriate course of action together).

People need to feel safe and secure before they can allow themselves to be vulnerable and say what they're really thinking. At the heart of *Short Christians* is a yearning for truthful expression between believers without fear of judgement or embarrassment, and hopefully your discussion times will open up opportunities for this honest exchange.

Author Notes

I've included author notes for each story towards the back of this edition, so that I can share with you what was on my heart as each story was created. I'd recommend that you read them before your group's session, as they'll really help you in leading the discussion times.

Reflections, Learning Points, Observations and Ideas...

After each story, there is some space for you to journal; if you are a small group leader, this will be valuable thinking space about how your group responded to the story. Here you can reflect on how a story has worked for your group, whether you ran the evening in the best format. You may have ideas for trying something new or how to develop things in the future. This is your private journaling space, and not something for you to share with your group.

Taking a few minutes the day after your group to reflect on how things went, and to think about what the evening taught you and how you might apply any lessons learned will feed you in your growth as a leader. I hope you'll find this section useful and rewarding, and that God will speak to you through the observations and thoughts you record here.

If you're a small group member, or are working through this book by yourself, use this space to jot down any thoughts that you didn't have room for in the *Let's Talk* section.

Finally

I hope you'll enjoy getting stuck into your *Short Christians* sessions as much as I've enjoyed writing them. I've seen how the stories have opened up discussions in my own small group, and beyond. My prayer is that they might bless your group as you read and discuss them together.

SAME TIME, SAME PLACE

*Sammi hosts the regular prayer group meeting
where needs are ignored while-u-wait*

The prayer circle met at their usual time (9:15am) on their usual day (Monday) at their usual place (Sammi's house), and, as usual, Marjorie arrived early. She was waiting on Sammi's doorstep when Sammi arrived home from the school run.

'Marjorie.' Sammi said the name with the same expressive quality she gave words like tea towel, vacuum cleaner or bleach. She rooted through her bag for her door key, and leaned to kiss the well-powdered cheek, feeling a tickle on the end of her nose from the dusty coating, her eyes simultaneously registering that the bin lid wasn't on properly.

Marjorie winced and stepped aside as Sammi reached towards the door, key dangerously close to eye level.

'I see your neighbours have started on the extension.' Marjorie slipped a hand into her coat pocket, double-checking that her own keys were still where she'd put them when she'd left home: increasingly she found that she was losing things. Marjorie was used to being the organised one, only suddenly she couldn't locate her diary when she needed it, and she had locked herself out of her flat twice on the weekend. Thankfully she kept a key with a neighbour, but knocking on their door and asking for help not once, but twice, was horribly humiliating and had shaken her up rather.

'A-ha!' Sammi pushed the door open with her foot, then leant back and checked her neighbours' houses on both sides to ensure no one was about and no windows were open. 'I was going to tell you about that. Definitely in vital need of prayer. I'll tell you when the others get here; save me repeating myself.'

Sammi took one last look left and one last look right, then stepped into the house. Marjorie followed.

'I thought you were going to redecorate your hallway last week?' Marjorie scrutinised the walls around her, thinking how drab Sammi's home was, how lacking in cosiness or colour. Considering Sammi was a stay-at-home mother, she didn't appear to spend any time on the actual home she stayed in, Marjorie thought (not for the first time).

'We were, but then we ended up having Catherine to stay –'

'Catherine?'

'You know, that girl at church who needed a few days between moving out of one flat and into another –' Sammi began shedding layers, dropping them onto the stairs.

Marjorie gazed at the piles of clothing, books, toys, school work, folded washing and goodness knew what else that lay strewn on every step of the stairs, and sighed.

'I don't know any Catherines at church,' she said.

'Well, you'd probably know her if you saw her. Anyway, she came to stay, and that meant we couldn't do anything about the hall, which was a shame but never mind, greater good and all that. She stayed in the lounge, which I'm sorry to say still smells slightly of sweaty plimsolls. Like I say, all for the greater good. We'll do the hallway next week. I know you're not keen on it.'

'What me? Oh, no, no, I like this green.' Marjorie hung her rain mac on one of the overloaded pegs behind the front door. It fell off. Sammi retrieved it and rammed it on to the peg, pulling Marjorie's favourite coat down hard until it stayed put. Marjorie ran a hand along the grubby wall and tried not to think about what damage might have been done to the lining of her coat. 'It's...restful on the eye. Sage, was it? When you first did it, I mean.'

'Clover. And you might as well enjoy it today, because this time next week it will be Poppy Field.' Sammi braced herself for Marjorie's reaction.

'Bright red? In a hallway?' Marjorie frowned.

'Warm red.' Sammi tried to sound patient, but heard the edge in her own voice.

'Blood red?' Marjorie winced.

'Rich red.' Sammi said firmly.

'Oh.'

'Coffee?' Sammi headed for the kitchen, her voice light again as she inwardly celebrated shutting Marjorie up. The doorbell pierced the air with its shrill ring.

'That'll be Franklin. I'll get it.' Marjorie turned and opened the door before Sammi could get to it.

'Miss Woods.' Franklin held out his hand.

'Franklin.' Marjorie sighed his name, clasped his hand in both of hers for a moment, then stepped aside, imagining this were her house, and Franklin was her husband, and here she was, welcoming him home. The first thing she'd do would be to get him to put some floral wallpaper up.

Franklin stepped in lightly –like a dancer, Marjorie thought – and removed his trilby hat.

'Always so smart,' Marjorie cooed.

'I wish everyone still wore hats,' Sammi called down from the kitchen. 'Coffee, Franklin?'

'Yes, please,' he replied, slipping his loafers off and swapping them for some slippers which he had brought with him in a plastic bag.

The door was still open when Gloria arrived.

'Morning all,' she called 'Ready to get on your knees?' She laughed, her blouse pulling dangerously tight across her large bosom as she did so. She stopped laughing, adjusted her shirt and touched her thick, black curls.

Franklin smiled. 'You're always such a breath of fresh air, Gloria' He stood, staring at her, taking in the wild colours of her nylon shirt, the bright pink flares and the platform heels.

'Yes, you certainly are fresh,' Marjorie said, her eyes fixed on Franklin.

'Is that another outfit from your fancy dress company?' Franklin blinked hard as his eyes adjusted to the brightness of Gloria's attire.

'No, Franklin.' Gloria frowned, 'This is something from my own wardrobe.'

'Oh, I'm terribly sorry.' Franklin blushed.

Gloria erupted into laughter. 'I'm joking, Frankie, I'm teasing you! Just ignore me, I'm playing with you, man!'

'Oh, I see.' Franklin tried to smile. 'Forgive me, I'm not so quick as you, Gloria.'

Marjorie tutted.

'Coffee, Gloria?' Sammi called from the kitchen.

'I'd love a redbush – I brought my own teabag,' Gloria called back.

Sammi took the tea bag, holding it by the string away from her body like it was a dead mouse.

'You three go through to the lounge and I'll be through in a minute with the drinks,' she said loudly over the hissing and bubbling of the electric kettle. 'And then we can get down to some serious praying,' she said, laughing.

The three sat in their usual seats; Gloria squishing her soft flesh against Marjorie's bony frame on the sofa, Franklin setting himself lightly in the armchair by the gas fire. Sammi came in with the drinks, set the wooden tray on the small coffee table between them all, plonked herself down on the beanbag, jerked violently, reached beneath her bottom and retrieved a *Lego* spaceship, then wriggled herself into a comfortable position.

Marjorie began the formalities. 'Well, now that we're all here, is there anything specific anyone would like prayer for?'

A moment's silence.

And another.

And another.

'Sammi, you mentioned your neighbour's extension?' Marjorie raised both eyebrows encouragingly.

'Oh, yes!' Sammi beamed, and the others sat up, poised to receive the latest development in this long-running street saga. 'Well, there's been a right fuss on the street this week.'

'A right fuss?' Marjorie frowned.

'Yes, you see, number twenty-eight hadn't read the planning permission notice properly, and have kicked up a stink about the whole thing, but number twenty-five are obviously beginning works now and the period for objections is past. Anyway, it's not like it's on their side of the road, but twenty-eight say they'll be the ones who'll have to look at it, and they'll lose the evening sun on their front room. Not that I've ever seen them sit in there, you never see number twenty-eight. They hide out in the back of their house.'

'Oh dear, yes, we should definitely pray.'

'Yes, we could pray for peace between neighbours, because things got really heated last night out there,' Sammi said.

'Heated?' Gloria reached for her tea.

'Number twenty-five called twenty-eight an effing idiot, and twenty-eight threatened legal action – I thought they were going to have an actual fight! The kids were out of bed, up at the windows saying 'Mum, mum, what's going on out there?' I sent Mike out in the end, to try and quieten them down, just for the sake of the children.'

'Gosh. So they didn't come to blows, then?' Gloria said.

'No, Mike poured oil on troubled waters.'

'Good old Mike,' Franklin said. 'Audrey was always so fond of him.'

'Mmmm.' Sammi smiled, and the four of them fell quiet a moment, remembering Franklin's wife.

'It must be coming up to the anniversary of Audrey...' Gloria took a slurp of tea.

'Last Friday,' Franklin said.

'Oh, Franklin, I'm sorry I missed the date,' Sammi said.

'Not to worry, not to worry. I'm just very glad to be able to take Audrey's place here in the prayer circle. It makes me feel closer to her, somehow, to know that I'm where she was.'

'Well it's lovely to have you.' Gloria reached out and touched Franklin's knee.

'Yes, lovely.' Marjorie reached out and touched the arm that Gloria was touching Franklin with.

'Thank you.' Franklin looked down at his shoes.

A moment's silence.

Gloria removed her hand from Franklin's knee, and Marjorie removed her hand from Gloria's arm.

'Gloria.' Marjorie turned in her seat. 'What news?'

'Any more internet matches?' Sammi giggled. 'Is there a romance we can pray into life?'

'Nothing lately, not since that crazy weirdo with the collection of olive pips from around the world.'

Gloria and Sammi laughed loudly, until Gloria snorted through her nose and Marjorie restored order.

'There must be something, Gloria. Working on the local paper must give you plenty of prayer material.'

'Not to mention your fancy dress website business,' Franklin added.

'Yes, thank you Franklin,' said Marjorie. 'There must be more going on in your life than that, Gloria?'

'Well, there is something that probably needs praying for, actually. And it is about the dating website.'

'Oh?' the others spoke as one, leaning in towards the coffee table in delicious anticipation.

'I was on there the other day and I couldn't help noticing that Deborah - you know, our church youth worker Deborah - has registered on the site. She's getting lots of interest, too.'

'Our Deborah? Well, I never!' Marjorie put her hand to her mouth. 'And on the internet, too!'

'Oh, there's no shame in online dating these days, Marjorie, everyone's at it. Only this week I noticed that both our church wardens are on one of those sites.' Sammi said. 'I wondered if they'd signed up together at the same time, or if it was just a coincidence.'

A pause.

'I was only on it to try and help a friend out,' she added.

'Well, it looks like we certainly must pray indeed. We must pray for the sort of young men who go trawling the internet looking for single ladies.' Marjorie adjusted the knees of her tights, pinching and teasing the orange nylon where it had twisted. Franklin shifted in his seat.

'Is it easy to register on one of these sites?' He pulled a little at the knot of his tie.

'Really easy,' Gloria gushed. 'If you've got a smart phone you can do it while you're waiting for the bus.'

'Waiting for the bus! Really!' Marjorie said, her eyes on Franklin.

'Do they have many...mature Christian ladies on these websites?' Franklin's voice was very light and controlled.

'Loads of 'em, Frankie my man,' Gloria laughed. 'I'll show you how to get on there later.'

'What would Audrey think?' Marjorie said.

'I'm sure Audrey would want Franklin to be happy,' Gloria said.

Franklin sank back into the armchair, and looked very small.

'I still miss Audrey, very much,' he said.

'Yes.' The replies came quickly from the three women. 'Of course you do,' and 'Such a wonderful woman.'

'And coming here makes me feel closer to her, a bit. To sit where she sat, and pray with you as she did. But when I go home, I'm alone again. The house is empty. It feels...empty.'

'Tell me about it.' Gloria reached over and touched Franklin's arm. Marjorie touched Gloria's arm.

They sat for a moment in silence, and then Sammi spoke.

'Are there any prayer requests for any of the men in the church, Franklin? I mean, do you know of anything we can pray for for them? Are any other men lonely? Or in trouble in some way?'

She took a large slurp of her coffee, spilling a little onto her skirt in her rush to get the cup to her lips.

'I'm not sure... let me see.' Franklin looked at the ceiling, wracking his brain for something.

'There must be someone,' Gloria chimed.

'Ah, yes, there is someone. I know that David Parish is having a very hard time at the moment.'

'In his work?' Gloria asked.

'In his marriage?' Marjorie asked.

'With his children?' Sammi asked.

'Actually it's with his mother. She's in a care home, and clearly nearing the end of her days. She isn't saved, and he's terribly worried about her. He's been praying for her for years, but without any external change.'

'Ah, I see.' Sammi put her cup down. 'Ok. Anything from you, Marjorie?'

Franklin felt the relief of attention switching away from him.

'Lots of things, I'm sure, but my mind's gone blank suddenly.' Marjorie pulled at her beads. 'The church has been buzzing this week with all the activity for the children's summer club going on.'

'What happened in the end between Jeanette and the man with the bouncy castle? I heard there'd been a big falling out,' Sammi said.

'Oh dear me, yes, it was dreadful,' Marjorie said, relieved to have something of interest to say. 'Well, you see, their rates have gone up this year, and we simply don't have the budget, but Paul had gone over Jeanette's head and made the booking, so Jeanette got presented with this enormous bill and rang the chap in a real temper! Let's just say we shan't be booking any more bouncy castles through *Big Fun Bouncers* anymore.'

'Well there's been quite a ruckus at school too, this week.' Sammi couldn't wait any longer.

'School?' Marjorie wasn't expecting to lose her timeslot quite so quickly.

'It seems that Karen McManus's eldest hasn't actually been to school for the last three weeks - unbeknown to Karen and John!'

'No!' Gloria said, beaming.

'Is that Duncan? Isn't he due to take his GCSEs this summer?'

'Yes, the exams actually began last week - and he's missed all of his so far.'

'That's so bad!' Gloria said.

'Karen must be mortified!' Marjorie said.

'And her a teacher!' Sammi said, hands held out, appealing to the group.

'Well, she went to work just weeks after they were born, you know. I know it's not fashionable, but in my day we stayed at home and cared for the children we'd chosen to have. And it will have an enormous impact on our society in years to come, you know, all these children who were handed over to strangers just days after they were born.' Marjorie pulled her cardigan around her shoulders.

'Well, it certainly sounds like they need some prayer.' Gloria said, 'Speaking of which - what time is it?'

'Ten thirty-eight,' Sammi read from her phone.

'Oh, I'm sorry – I'm going to have to go – I've got a work meeting at eleven.' Gloria heaved herself up from the soft sofa, and headed for the hall to retrieve her coat.

Sammi rolled out of the beanbag, onto all fours on the carpet, and groaned as she got up from there.

Franklin stood, and began to straighten his shirt and tie.

'You going, too?' Sammi asked.

'Yes, I've got a doctor's appointment at eleven-fifteen,' he murmured.

'Nothing serious, I hope,' said Sammi, going to the hallway to open the door for Gloria as she left.

Marjorie stood and picked up her neat, black handbag, checking that everything was still there. She went to the hallway, slipped her coat on, and checked her pocket one more time for her keys.

'Thank you, Sammi, thanks for the coffee.'

'My pleasure,' said Sammi, waving to Gloria as she disappeared down the path, calling goodbyes over her shoulder.

Marjorie considered waiting for Franklin to be ready to leave: she had no plans today, and no desire to be in her own company. She had no plans for tomorrow, either. She wouldn't be in the church office until Wednesday, and that seemed a very long, empty time away from right now.

Franklin wasn't moving very fast, though.

'Goodbye, then,' Marjorie said, and left, patting the keys in her pocket.

Franklin stepped into the hall, once he'd heard Marjorie's farewell. He pulled his coat on, and popped his hat lightly on top of his head.

'Nice to see you, Sammi,' he said, and kissed her lightly on the cheek. He put one foot out of the house and onto the doormat, and then he paused, wondering whether he might say something to Sammi after all about the reason for his doctor's appointment.

'You too, Franklin,' Sammi said, and began closing the door – a little too quickly: she caught his heel. Not realising that it was Franklin himself who was causing the obstruction, she yanked the door open before trying to shut it again, hard. Franklin was rubbing the back of his leg at the time, soothing the pain caused by the swing of the door.

This time he cried out as the door hit his knuckles, crushing his fingers between his soft calf and the hard wood.

'Oh, I'm so sorry, Franklin! I didn't see you there,' Sammi said.

'No matter, my dear, my fault,' said Franklin, swallowing hard. 'I should have said something.'

He lifted his leg away from the door, raised his hat politely, then turned and walked down the path, letting the tears that he'd been blinking back find their way to his cheeks.

'See you next week, Franklin,' Sammi called. 'Same time, same place.'

LET'S TALK

1.   How is prayer misused in this story?

_____

_____

_____

_____

2.   What do you think got in the way of each group member *actually praying*? What held them back from sharing what was really going on in their lives?

_____

_____

_____

_____

3.   When Franklin is asked for prayer requests for the men in the church, the answer he gives disappoints the women in the group: 'Actually it's with his mother. She's in a care home, and clearly nearing the end of her days. She isn't saved, and he's terribly worried about her. He's been praying for years for her, but without change.'
'Ah, I see,' Sammi put her cup down. 'Ok. Anything from you, Marjorie?'
Franklin felt the relief of attention switching away from him...'
Do you feel we pray with enough urgency for those who don't know Jesus?

_____

_____

_____

_____

4. How do you think you could build up a group where prayer needs are expressed openly, honestly and safely, as and when people need?

_____

_____

_____

_____

5. What makes a *good* time of prayer together for you?

_____

_____

_____

_____

6. What makes a less satisfying prayer time together?

_____

_____

_____

_____

7. How could your group spend more time intentionally listening for God's voice together?

_____

_____

_____

_____

LET'S LISTEN

'In prayer there is a connection between what God does and what you do. You can't get forgiveness from God, for instance, without also forgiving others. If you refuse to do your part, you cut yourself off from God's part.'

Matthew 6:14-15

'I urge you to pray for absolutely everything, ranging from small to large...'

Matthew 18:19-20

'You're blessed when you get your inside world – your mind and heart – put right. Then you can see God in the outside world.'

Matthew 5:8

'The world is full of so-called prayer warriors who are prayer-ignorant. They're full of formulas and programmes and advice, peddling techniques for getting what you want from God. Don't fall for that nonsense. This is your Father you're dealing with, and he knows better than you what you need. With a God like this loving you, you can pray very simply...'

Matthew 6:7-10

LET'S PRAY

This seems to be an ideal opportunity to pray - about prayer!

❖ Pour your struggles with prayer out to God, and ask for his help. Ask him to lead you into prayer naturally as a small group, and also to help you persist when you feel too tired to pray and you'd all rather go home and get to bed.

❖ Ask for sensitivity and creativity, so that your group may look for new opportunities and ways to pray, and for willing hearts to listen for God's voice for one another.

❖ Prayer really can build your group like nothing else: together we can try hard and make small changes (which often don't last) but when we turn to God and confess our need for him and proclaim our dependence upon him, that's when he can get stuck in and really change things. Relationships are built and healed, characters are grown, and we get to see a little more of God's kingdom come into our daily lives.

PRAYER JOURNAL SPACE

_____

_____

_____

_____

_____

_____

_____

_____

_____

REFLECTIONS, LEARNING POINTS AND IDEAS FROM THIS SESSION...

DOUBLE FIGURES

*Ruby's growing up in a Christian family,
and learning the rules as she goes.*

It's my birthday, so I wake up extra early and climb into Mum and Dad's bed. I have to scramble over their legs and snuffle my way under the duvet between them. Dad's elbow is right in my ear. Mum groans and says 'How come I have to drag you out of bed for school but you have no problem waking early on the weekend?' I laugh and roll around madly between Mum and Dad some more, even though it means my nose keeps bumping into Dad's elbow. I can't help it; I'm happy.

Today I am ten years old: double figures at last!

'Can I open my presents now?'

'Wait for your brother to get up.'

Ugh. Benji's so slow at getting up. Mum says he'd sleep till lunch given the chance. But I can't wait till lunch, I need to get on with my birthday, and it's already – I need to check Dad's clock to find out...Dad says 'Oof!' as I have to climb over him to see it and my elbow digs into his tummy. He's curled up like a hedgehog now. 'Happy birthday, Ruby,' he wheezes. He looks like he might cry.

'Thank you, Daddy.' I kiss his nose and he smiles but he stays all scrunched up in a ball.

'What's the time, Mr Wolf?' he groans.

'Six twenty-four and a half,' I say.

'Ah,' says Mummy, 'then it's not your official birthday yet. You were born at six forty-two.'

'No!' I shout and throw myself back over them.

This is heaven. Me, Dad and Mum in the Big Bed. No Benji. Just me. This is the life! I'm in no rush for presents, suddenly. I just want to lie here for the day, just the three of us.

Mum fidgets.

'Cup of tea?' she asks Dad.

'I'll do it,' he says, and rolls out of bed. He heads downstairs, still walking sort of curled over from the tummy jab I gave him before. Mum and me lie there listening as he fills the kettle from the kitchen tap and flicks it on. He goes to the downstairs loo and wees for so long it sounds like he's running a bath. He farts. Dad always farts in the kitchen, like he thinks no one can hear him in there. I'm not supposed to say 'farts' out loud. I'm supposed to say 'wind,' or I can say 'pops' so I sound like either a very old person or a baby. I can even combine those two to make 'windy-pops,' which makes me sound like a baby-ish old person, but I don't have to use any words right at this moment: we both heard it, so I just say the word in my head: Dad's farty-farty-farted. Mum and me look at each other and then we start giggling, and she doesn't even know that I'm saying FART over and over inside my head.

It's going to be a great day. I can feel it.

And then I hear Benji's bed creak. He's moving about.

'Dad's fart's woken up Benji,' I say, and I'm struggling to get the words out between giggles.

'Ruby.' Mum's raising an eyebrow at me in warning, but she's still smiling.

Benji shuffles in, rubbing his eyes and dragging his blankie on the floor.

'Good morning, sweetheart,' says Mum, reaching for him. She didn't reach for me when I came in. I tell her so in my baby voice.

'That's because I was still asleep when you came in,' she says, and she's still raising that eyebrow at me.

'Whatever,' I say.

'Ruby!' She's suddenly sitting up and now she's frowning. 'We don't say *Whatever* to each other in this house.'

'Soz.'

She frowns in a way that says 'We don't say *soz*, either'.

'Sorry,' I mumble. Honestly, you'd think they'd make some allowances for my birthday wouldn't you?

Benji climbs in Dad's side and snuggles up to me. He kisses my cheek.

'It's your birthday,' he says.

For a millisecond I think it's not so bad having a five year old brother and it's even maybe quite nice really, and then Benji throws his leg across me and starts elbowing my guts and I see that he is really only trying to get past me to get next to Mum. At least having a brother means an extra present from him, I suppose. *Whatever.*

Dad's back with the tea and now that we're all awake, I'm allowed to open my presents.

'It's six forty-four now, so you're officially two minutes old,' says Mum, pulling cards out from her bedside table and dropping them onto the bed.

There are only two packages.

'It's just cards,' I say.

'That's what happens as you get older, Ruby-Roo,' says Dad. 'You wait until you're forty-five. You're just grateful that anybody remembers you at all.'

Mum says, 'Ahhh, Tony,' and reaches across the pillows and rubs his hair.

'Shall I help you?' Benji reaches for a package. I grab it.

'No thank you. I am ten years old and I think I am quite able to open a parcel for myself by now.'

I tear at the paper before he can get his greedy little fingers back on it, and then I see the present and I just have to slump and hmph.

'Another piggy bank! That means I've got five piggy banks now and no money to put in any of them! I should open a shop and sell my piggy banks and then I might have some money instead!'

'Now, Ruby, come on,' says Dad, 'that's very thoughtful of Auntie Jo to send you that.'

'Yeah.' Mum puts on her American voice. 'Let's have an attitood of gratitood, young lady.' She's smiling. I bet she agrees with me really, but grown-ups have to pretend to be happy when they're not all the time and they have to be polite when they want to say the truth instead.

The other parcel is nail polish from my Godmother, Katy. I'm dead pleased but Mum and Dad make a big deal about how I can only put it on in the bathroom, never in a room with a carpet and I can't wear it out anywhere because I'm 'only ten' (which is weird, coz just half an hour ago they couldn't believe HOW OLD I was!), and it's not a good idea especially for school or church, and mum says none of the other girls at church wear nail polish, although she did see Esther Bradley with pink lip gloss on last week and was very surprised because Esther's mum is a Deacon but anyway, that's none of our business and something for them to work out.

'Of course what I'm really wanting is the guinea pigs.'

'We know,' says Dad, 'but you must remember that they're very expensive. We've asked all the family to put money in for your guinea pig fund, so let's see what's in those cards, eh?'

I start on the cards, which is a tricky business with my little brother around.

'No, Benji,' it's MY birthday, not yours.' I have to keep reminding him. Five year olds! They have terrible memories for good behaviour!

There was twenty pounds in the first card from Grandpa and Granny-Sue, then another ten pounds in the card from Nanna. Uncle Pete had sent fifteen pounds and Uncle James had sent twenty-five! Every card I opened had money in it!

'The guinea pigs and their hutch cost one hundred and fifty-five pounds altogether,' says Dad. 'How much money do you have?'

I count up the notes. I can't believe it: I count again.

'Let me help,' Mum says. We count them together.

I have exactly one hundred and fifty-five pounds!

Exactly!

'God must want you to have those guinea pigs, too!' Mum says.

The phone rings. I race downstairs.

'It'll be for me,' I call as I run.

And you might just think I've got a magic gift of telling the future, because it is for me. Well, I suppose it's pretty obvious really, it being my birthday and all that. Anyway, it's Nanna.

Mum comes into the lounge behind me. 'Don't forget to say thank you for the ten pounds,' she whispers.

I say, 'Nanna, you won't believe it, I needed one hundred and fifty-five pounds for the guinea pigs.'

'Ooh, that's a lot of money,' she says. Nanna thinks the price of everything is shocking, so her reaction doesn't come as any surprise to me.

'Yes, Nanna, but I got EXACTLY one hundred and fifty-five pounds for my birthday!'

'Did you?'

'Tell her everyone chipped in,' Mum says over my shoulder.

'It was from everyone chipping,' I repeat.

'That's amazing,' says Nanna.

'Mum said God must want me to have those guinea pigs, too,' I say.

'I believe she's right,' says Nanna. 'You must remember to thank God.'

'And thank Nanna, too!' Mum's lips are right in my ear and it really tickles in a horrible itchy way.

'Oh, yes, and thank you too, Nanna. I can't wait to get the guinea pigs! I hope we'll go today. I wish you lived nearer, you could come with us.'

'I wish so too, Ruby, but I'll see you soon, and I'll look forward to hearing all about your new furry friends when we next speak.'

'Okay.'

'God bless.' She makes a kiss sound. 'Is Mummy there?'

I give the phone to Mum. 'She wants to speak to you,' I whisper, and go upstairs to try out some nail polishes on Benji.

Mum's already saying 'I know, praise the Lord! Isn't God amazing?!'

I paint Benji's nails in stripes: blue, purple and yellow. He likes them. Dad isn't too happy. I hear him muttering something about having words with Katy about it all, but I know he won't do that. We don't have any nail polish remover, so Benji's got to stay this way for a while.

At half past ten, the door goes. I can tell it's Granny-Sue from her special knock – duhduhduhduhduh - duhduh!

'I'll get it,' I announce. I pull the door open wide.

'Oh my God, you've grown another foot, I swear, since last week!'

'Hello, Sue.' Dad comes down the hallway. He gives her that funny hug he always gives her, like he somehow manages to hug her without actually touching her.

Granny-Sue grabs Dad's chin.

'When are you gonna shave that beard off? Ya big hairy monster!'

Dad hates it when Granny-Sue goes on about his beard. Especially when she gets hold of his chin.

'Is Dad out there?' Dad says, looking over Granny-Sue's shoulder. It's funny to think of Grandpa as being Dad's Dad. It's funny to think about Dad even having a Dad.

'Ah, you know your Dad, Tony. He's carrying out a detailed inspection of the street on his way from the car.'

Dad pokes his head out of the front door. I go out onto the path. Sure enough, Grandpa is leaning over next door's fence.

'They want to treat that lawn,' he says to me.

'Grandpa, I'm ten years old.' I say, 'Don't talk to me about lawns!'

'You cheeky wee bugger,' he says, and he gives me a cuddle. It's like that with Grandpa, he likes me to make jokes with him. I'm the only one allowed to do it. He gets cross if anyone else does it. Benji doesn't dare. He's dead scared of Grandpa. He won't admit it, but I know the truth. You don't get to ten years old without learning a thing or two along the way.

'Gordon, come on in.' Mum's here. I hope she didn't hear Grandpa say bugger; she doesn't like it when he talks like that. He always talks like that.

'Come on, then.' Grandpa holds out his hand. 'Come on and show me what you got for your birthday.'

I take Grandpa inside.

Granny-Sue's having a cup of tea, and Grandpa has one too. We sit at the table.

'So,' says Grandpa, 'what did you get, Ruby-Roo?'

It's the moment I've been waiting for. I race upstairs to collect my pile of money. Benji's taken some and I find it under his pillow and give him a quick thump. He stays quiet because he knows Mum'll be furious if she finds out he stole.

I take the cash downstairs and I make a fancy show of spreading it out on the table, note by note.

'We were wondering where you'd got to,' says Mum.

'O.M.G,' says Granny-Sue.

'We don't say that,' Benji says from somewhere behind me. He's come downstairs to sulk about the money. I give him a look to remind him that I know he stole and I'll be saving that information for some other, more useful moment: he sticks his tongue out at me when no one's looking at him. *Whatever.*

'Oooh!' says Granny-Sue to Benji, in a funny posh voice, 'Don't you, dahhhhling?'

'Well, Benji, that's ok, we don't tell other people what to say,' Mum says quietly to Benji.

'But it means –'

'I know,' Mum cuts in quick, 'but it might just mean 'Oh my goodness,' or 'Oh my gosh,' and it's up to other people how they speak.'

'Yes, Benji,' I say, 'it's none of our business and something for them to work out.'

Benji sticks his thumb in his mouth and stares at Granny-Sue. Mum gets up from the table and excuses herself. She's probably gone for a poo (she always does one in the morning) but I don't say it. I would have definitely said something when I was nine, but I guess I must be maturing or something, because there's no way I'm risking saying anything about poo right now.

'Come on then, how much did you get?' Grandpa says.

'Well, you won't believe this, Grandpa. The guinea pigs and their hutch cost one hundred and fifty-five pounds altogether, and guess how much I got?'

'Twenty-five million,' he says.

'Ooh, can I have some?' says Granny-Sue.

'Yeah, we'd better crack open the champers,' says Grandpa.

'No, no,' I say. I'm a bit annoyed because now it won't sound so much money when I say it.

'Grandpa's just having fun with you, Ruby. Go on, tell him how much you got. Dad rubs my shoulders. Everyone's listening to me again AT LAST.

'I only got exactly a hundred and fifty-five pounds, Grandpa!'

'No way!'

'Exactly!'

'God, that's - I mean, gosh - that's amazing!' says Granny-Sue, and I can tell she's totally gobsmacked.

'It's like God –' and then I remember, Granny-Sue and Grandpa don't go to church. 'I'm really lucky,' I say, and Dad smiles at me, and our eyes say to each other, 'That was a close one!'

'I'll say,' says Grandpa. 'Sounds like someone up there is smiling down on you.' I look at the ceiling. I can hear Mum's footsteps up there. I wonder if she is smiling down on me just now.

'OMG,' says Granny-Sue. It goes quiet for a second. 'As in Oh my goodness,' she says. Dad laughs.

And this is the moment when Benji does an explosive fart. We're all laughing so hard, except Benji who's cross with us, but that just makes it funnier, and then Grandpa has a sneezing fit and his sneezes are so funny that even Benji starts laughing, and the laughing makes him fart again. I have to hold my tummy, it's starting to hurt.

'OMG!' I say, and Granny-Sue does a snort laugh, which really gets me rolling on the floor, laughing so much I'm crying. Then I see Mum's come back into the kitchen and her eyebrow is raised at me and I stop laughing.

LET'S TALK

1. In this story, how do you think this double-way of speaking is shaping Ruby's thoughts and ideas growing up?

    _____

    _____

    _____

    _____

2. What do you think would have happened if the family had spoken with their non-Christian relatives in the same way they spoke to each other and their Nanna?

    _____

    _____

    _____

    _____

3. What was your family culture like with regards to the way you spoke and the language that was ok to use at home when you were growing up?

    _____

    _____

    _____

    _____

4. Did you grow up in a Christian family? If so, did your family have many non-Christian friends or relatives?

    _____

    _____

    _____

5. If you didn't grow up in a Christian family, do you remember the first Christians you met? Were you aware of any differences in the language or culture between you and them?

    _____

    _____

    _____

    _____

6. In what ways do you find you change the way you talk about things depending on who you're talking to?

    _____

    _____

    _____

    _____

7. Imagine Ruby as an adult: how do you think she might look back on being raised in a Christian home, based on this brief episode?

    _____

    _____

    _____

    _____

LET'S LISTEN

'Let me tell you why you are here. You're here to be salt-seasoning that brings out the God-flavours of this earth. If you lose your saltiness, how will people taste godliness?'

Matthew 5:13a

'Don't worry about what you'll say or how you'll say it. The right words will be there; the spirit of your Father will supply the words. When people realise it is the living God you are presenting and not some idol that makes them feel good, they are going to turn on you, even people in your own family. There is a great irony here: proclaiming so much love, experiencing so much hate! But don't quit. Don't cave in. It is all well worth it in the end...'

Matthew 10:17-22

'Don't be bluffed into silence by the threats of bullies. There's nothing they can do to your soul, your core being. Save your fear for God, who holds your entire life - body and soul - in his hands.'

Matthew 10:28

'If any of you are embarrassed over me and the way I'm leading you when you get around your fickle and unfocused friends, know that you'll be an even greater embarrassment to the Son of Man when he arrives in all the splendour of God, his father, with an army of the holy angels.

Mark 8:38

This last verse is very hard-hitting: don't be afraid to face it,
wrestle with it, pray about it and explore it further.

LET'S PRAY

Think about specific relationships you have where you perhaps struggle to feel free to express your faith naturally and openly.

❖ Pray for one another about these relationships and about the fear or hesitation you may feel within them when it comes to expressing your faith.

❖ Pray about any other issues raised by your group's discussion today.

PRAYER JOURNAL SPACE

_____

_____

_____

_____

_____

_____

_____

_____

_____

_____

_____

_____

_____

_____

_____

_____

_____

_____

REFLECTIONS, LEARNING POINTS AND IDEAS FROM THIS SESSION...

YOURS FAITHFULLY

Eva Bishop's letter to her vicar in response
to his sermon on emotional maturity.

D<small>ear</small> Vicar,

I'm writing to thank you so much for this morning's service and in particular your sermon about emotional maturity. What a timely message, so true and useful for the church. (I didn't get much from the worship, mind you).

The things you said about emotional maturity really struck a chord with me.

It's all too easy to appear qualified as a fully-fledged, proper Christian while in reality remaining a spiritual infant. I only hope your words reached the right ears as, let's face it, there are many in our congregation who need to hear them desperately. I'm sure you know the <u>particular individuals</u> I'm referring to.

When you said the prayer at the end, I was praying it with all my strength for Connie McGuire (sitting next to me) who often seems frighteningly out of control of her emotions for someone in her - well, I'd guess late 40s - what would you say? Perhaps early 50s? (Either way, she's certainly at least ten years too old for that tattoo on her left ankle.) I have, in recent months, watched her crying <u>again and again</u> during times of worship, and she's always going up for prayer in floods of tears like a teenager, or <u>worse.</u> I worry about the message she sends out to others – she's clearly out of control.

And when you talked about how people in church need to think before speaking lest they cause some offence, my mind flew immediately to that chap who often wears his orange bobble hat during services. You know the one – Phil is it? Or Dave? Phil or Dave, one of those names – Steve? Is it Steve? I've lost count of the number of times he has said offensive things to me – I think it's up to seven, now.

Once, I took a woman's cup away (I was on coffee duty <u>again</u> and I needed to wash up – this is another issue that you could do with addressing, actually, vicar: people <u>will talk</u>, on and on at the end of church. It makes it very difficult for those of us trying to leave the hall in a tidy state for the Brownies' Monday meeting. Perhaps we could have some sort of 'five minute conversation' limit imposed? Anything longer and they need to take it out into the car park. Better for everyone, especially anyone trapped with Phyllis Duggan.) Anyway, this woman had left it too late to drink up, so I took the church's cup from out of her hand in order to go and wash it up. I had quite a job to pull our cup from her grasp, so I said, 'It's drink up or wash up time! Rules is rules,' I said! Well, they are, aren't they?

Well! <u>He</u> – Phil, Dave or Steve or whoever he is, you know who I mean, don't you, orange bobble hat person – <u>he</u> grabbed the cup from me and gave it back to the woman, I think she was a visitor for a baptism or something, and he said 'I don't think so, Eva!' Those were his <u>actual words</u>! Just like <u>that</u>!

I have no idea what happened to that woman's cup in the end – I only hope Phil, Dave or Steve – or is it Chris? – Anyway, I just hope he took responsibility for his actions and washed it up himself. Somehow, I doubt it.

We can only hope God changes his heart and his outlook, and that in the meantime God might protect those of us whom he offends so freely.

And then there's Tony and Marissa with the new baby. I know it's their first but, really, talk about a pair of drama queens! I mean, millions of people have babies every day - what's the big deal?!

I for one didn't know where to look last week when Marissa started breastfeeding right there in the church! Right in front of all of us! <u>Breast</u>feeding! With <u>men</u> and <u>children</u> in the same room!

Imagine if the second coming had happened on Sunday and she'd been caught out in that position! Or if we'd had a fire alarm! Or the BBC had turned up to film an impromptu episode of Songs of Praise! It doesn't bear thinking about.

And what damage is she doing to young impressionable minds? (Or old ones, for that matter?) What's wrong with a bottle, I want to know? I was bottle-fed. Everyone was bottle-fed when I was a baby, I'm certain of it.

I saw that sticker up by the doors saying we are a 'breastfeeding friendly church,' and of course I realise that God designed this mode of feeding for those emergency situations when there's no bottle to hand, but it's entirely possible to be friendly to people whilst putting them in a room with a door that we can close.

The simple fact is, it's very difficult to sing, pray, read or listen to the sermon when there is an appendage exposed. I didn't know where to look during 'When I Survey.'

And the fuss her husband makes of the baby! Honestly, it's just a baby! Put it down, let it cry - we all have to accept sooner or later that no one's going to give us attention just because we're awake! The earlier in life that lesson's learnt, the better, I believe.

Your words were like arrows shooting straight to the pair of them. I only hope they looked up from the baby long enough to hear what you said.

And what about our newest newly-weds? I slipped into the back row of their wedding just a month ago. All that money spent on the reception - I heard all about it - and what did I see in the church car park, just one day after they returned from their honeymoon? There were the supposed lovebirds having a right old humdinger in that rusty Honda Civic of hers! Who knows how long they'll last? It's hardly a good start, is it? I mean, Christian marriage is there to be a reflection of the glory of God: I'd hardly call a row in a Honda Civic a joyous echo of our Creator's splendour, would you?

The problem with married people is it all comes too easy for them. They want to try being single for forty seven years, then they wouldn't be so despising of their good fortune. They take it for granted, forgetting how lonely everyone else is.

Before I sign off, I wanted to explain my recent absence, and quash any rumours you may have heard regarding it. I know how quickly gossip and wrong assumptions fly around this church. 'One should never assume,' my mother used to say, and how right she was! A certain somebody - I won't name them, but you do know them (they've got red hair) - asked me if I might be depressed last week (and they drive a Volvo) when I bumped into them in Sainsbury's, and if that might be why I hadn't been at church for a while. (They've got a Labrador).

I'd like to set the record straight on this one: there's absolutely totally and utterly nothing wrong with me! I was just not at my best, that's all, and I always feel it's better not to come to church when one's not feeling at one's best, because nobody needs to be dragged down by another's whinging and whining - it's not helpful to the church. This is why you haven't seen me - I've been waiting until I am better again, so that I may cheerfully encourage those around me. Just the sort of spiritual maturity you're looking for, am I right?

I must draw to a close. I've got my neighbour coming in. She's had a terrible time of it, poor woman, lost her husband six months ago. She's entirely unable to cope, so I'm doing my bit. Mind you, she's not an easy woman, it's no wonder people steer clear of her. I couldn't get anyone else from the street to join us for coffee. Still, thank goodness I'm here, at least there's some Christian witness going on in my neighbourhood. I shall raise her spirits, if only for a little while. If nothing else, I shall thank God for the reminder that there's always someone worse off than yourself. My mother used to say that, too - how right she was!

Yours faithfully,

Eva Bishop

LET'S TALK

1. What are Eva's complaints? List them out. What does each one tell us about what's really going on in Eva's life?

    _____

    _____

    _____

    _____

2. 'It's all too easy to appear qualified as a fully-fledged, proper Christian while remaining a spiritual infant...' What do you think about this assertion of Eva's at the beginning of her letter?

    _____

    _____

    _____

    _____

3. Compose a letter from the vicar in response to Eva's letter. What will you say to her?

    _____

    _____

    _____

    _____

    _____

    _____

    _____

    _____

    _____

4. How do you deal with the temptation to apply God's word to others and not to yourself?

_____

_____

_____

_____

_____

5. Do you feel you know those you share church life with beyond a Sunday service? How does / can your church deepen understanding, empathy, love and support between members?

_____

_____

_____

_____

_____

_____

LET'S LISTEN

'Our Father is kind; you be kind.

'Don't pick on people, jump on their failures, criticise their faults – unless, of course, you want the same treatment. Don't condemn those who are down; that hardness can boomerang. Be easy on people; you'll find life a lot easier...

Luke 6:36-37

'Here is a simple, rule-of-thumb guide for behaviour. Ask yourself what you want people to do for you, then grab the initiative and do it for them...'

Matthew 7:12

'Let me tell you something: Every one of these careless words is going to come back to haunt you. There will be a time of Reckoning. Words are powerful; take them seriously. Words can be your salvation. Words can also be your damnation.'

Matthew 12:36-37

'So where does that leave you when you criticize a brother? And where does that leave you when you condescend to a sister? I'd say it leaves you looking pretty silly – or worse. Eventually we're all going to end up kneeling side by side in the place of judgment, facing God. Your critical and condescending ways aren't going to improve your position there one bit...'

Romans 14:11

LET'S PRAY

❖ Pray together in response to any issues raised by this evening's discussion.

❖ You might like to take your letter writing further, and write your prayers as letters to God this evening, to be shared or not as is considered appropriate.

PRAYER JOURNAL SPACE

_____

_____

_____

_____

_____

_____

_____

_____

_____

_____

_____

_____

_____

_____

_____

_____

_____

_____

_____

REFLECTIONS, LEARNING POINTS AND IDEAS FROM THIS SESSION...

BACK IN THE DAYS WHEN THE PICTURES CAME

*For years, Sharon's testimony and prophetic words meant that
she enjoyed near-celebrity status in her church,
but lately God seems to have gone quiet on her...*

'Is everything alright, darling? Only, I suddenly realised in church this morning that you haven't been up to the front during worship for ages.' Jonathan handed Sharon the crystal sherry glass and leaned back against the Aga, enjoying the warmth spreading through the back of his smooth linen trousers.

'Mmm.' Sharon turned her back on him and frowned at the lamb joint in the roasting tin before her. A bunch of rosemary, freshly picked from the garden, lay beside it, and she pulled some of the hard, sharp leaves away from the woody stem and stabbed them hard into the mottled, fatty flash.

'Ah! Now I know there's definitely something wrong.' Jonathan stepped towards where his wife stood at the kitchen island unit. He put his sherry down and rubbed her shoulders lightly, hoping to soothe. But Sharon's shoulders began to shake, and sobs broke loose before she could catch them and hold them in.

'Come on, now.' He turned her towards him and she buried her face in his shoulder. 'What's going on?'

Now that she'd begun, Sharon wept hard, her tears running down Jonathan's neck and pooling in the hollow of his collarbone, her mascara smearing on his crisp white shirt. She rubbed at the wet that was running from her nose to her lip and tried to regain control.

'It's all gone wrong,' she whispered.

'Wrong?' Jonathan smoothed her hair, kissed her cheek, lifted her chin and brought her eyes to meet his. 'What's gone wrong?'

'The pictures have stopped coming,' she blurted the words between sobs. Jonathan gently ran his hands over her back, following the bumps of her spine to its base. Sharon pulled away.

'I've had so many over this last year – so many! And they've all been spot on, you know? All of them. Every week someone's come up to me after the service and said, *"That word was for me, Sharon,"* and *"Thanks, Sharon - that meant so much"* – every week, without fail. But recently – well, like you say – I haven't been up the front for a while. There's simply nothing happening. I pray, I wait – and nothing comes.'

'Perhaps God's giving you a break.' Jonathan smiled, then saw this wasn't the response she wanted. 'Hey, listen.' He looked at her, his face serious now. 'I've *never* had a picture to take up the front. It's normal *not* to have pictures, as far as I can make out. I've been a Christian for thirty years now, and as far as I can see it's entirely normal to never hear from God at all. You really were quite *abnormal* in having so many and hearing so often, you know.'

'It's just always been that way for me, ever since that night on the Alpha course. The moment I gave my life to Christ the pictures just started coming.'

'But you've so much to be thankful for.' Jonathan reached again for his sherry. 'Never mind if you have a picture or not, it's not like it's your job or anything, you're not under contract to bring a picture every Sunday. Perhaps your new role is to sit with your husband and relax.'

'Mmm.' Sharon turned back to the lamb joint. The conversation was over, and Jonathan turned his attentions to the cat mewing next to its empty food bowl.

***

The next Sunday, it happened again, which is to say, nothing happened. Sharon sat throughout the worship time, shifting on her plastic seat, waiting for something to come, willing something to come, whilst simultaneously feeling that in the desperate waiting she was beginning to somehow block anything that might come, rather like a child waiting up to see the tooth fairy: no fairy would come as long as she was straining to catch a glimpse of silken wing.

Two teenagers from the youth group shared words which cut Sharon deep. *Teenagers!* What experience did they have of life? She'd actually *lived*.

There was no doubt amongst the congregation that Sharon had lived. Her testimony was the stuff of legend in the church. It got rolled out at regular intervals, she spoke at the Alpha course every year about her life transforming conversion experience. People sat gripped, mouths open, eyes wide when she spoke about the changes in her life.

She always began with the violence, the abuse that she'd suffered for two decades in silence. Then she went on to the gulf that had formed between her and her wayward daughter, Gemma. She moved on to Gemma's drug-taking, teenage pregnancy and estrangement. She spoke of her own unhappiness, loneliness, anti-depressants and fear.

And then she changed the pace, and watched her audience's faces catch onto the glimmer of hope on the horizon of her story: the day she'd wandered into church when she was supposed to be going to pick up the Sunday papers for her husband. The fear she'd felt as she'd crept in, and the welcome she'd received that had melted that fear like magic.

She told them about how she'd kept coming back, and back and back. How her husband was too hung-over on a Sunday morning to clock what was going on. How Sundays became her solace, her escape, her hope.

And then she'd heard of the daytime Alpha course, and she knew she would just die if she didn't go. She'd found ways, lying, sneaking, desperately deceiving ways to get to be at that Alpha course every week.

She'd handed her life over willingly, with relief – 'God could take it,' she told them, 'coz I sure didn't want my life. I wanted the life God had for me. From the moment I took that step,' she would almost whisper, watching their faces absorbing the visible effects of her words, 'everything changed.'

She loved seeing their expressions as she told them of her escape from the house where she had been a victim for all those years. It got even better when she told them that she'd been able to divorce her violent husband peacefully. Then, when she told them she'd met a true gentleman in the church who loved her just as she was, she felt the emotion in the room swelling. The women on the Alpha course would wipe their eyes and sniff, smiling at her and hopeful for themselves.

But it got even better when she revealed to them that her once-nasty ex-husband had actually gone on to confront his behaviour and had been through counselling. When she told them of his subsequent conversion and joining the church they often applauded. And when they discovered that he was serving in the kitchen for them that very evening - well, he usually got brought out and given a standing ovation.

But she saved the *pièce de resistance* until the end, introducing her daughter as one of the course leaders, and producing a photo of Ruby, the granddaughter she now enjoyed a close relationship with.

She had come to realise that she was an evangelist's dream come true.

On top of that, God seemed to be flooding her senses with imagery: imagery that spoke to the broken, the downhearted, the lost and weary; those who filled the chairs every week desperate for God to speak into their lives.

Some people even travelled distances to the church to hear the words she would bring. Her next door neighbours heard about her through friends of theirs and came to see for themselves. They'd come to faith that day, on the strength of a picture she brought, and were now embedded in church life, helping with the running of the youth group.

There was no doubt about it amongst the congregation: Sharon had the Hotline To God ringing off the hook.

So why the silence now?

***

'It was nice to have you next to me throughout the service this morning.' Jonathan tried a different track back home, after church. He poured the sherry carefully, enjoying the sensation of the cat wrapping itself around his legs in anticipation of a feed.

The violent clanging of pots and pans from the kitchen island unit let him know he'd said the wrong thing.

***

When Sharon wasn't asked to speak at the Alpha course that term, she knew why: she was no longer delivering the goods.

No one had spoken to her about not doing it; they'd simply asked someone else. Worse than that, they'd asked *Lola*.

Lola was new to the church. She'd been on the last Alpha course. She'd been a Jehovah's Witness or a Mormon or something like that (Sharon could never remember which) before coming to Alpha. Sharon felt she should be able to remember, because they went on about it at church often enough, but for some reason there was a block there in her memory.

Lola put the chairs away in the most irritatingly nice way at the end of the service each week. There was just something about her manner: *showy*. Other people seemed blind to it, like the sun shone out of her backside every time she bent to stack another chair, Sharon thought as she studied her.

During the worship that Sunday morning, Sharon stayed seated. She tightened every muscle in her body; she clenched her jaw and held her eyelids closed so that they caused a sort of under-water noise to drone in her ears.

Nothing came.

The worship just wasn't moving her lately. It wasn't getting to her like it used to, back in the days when the pictures came. Perhaps that was the problem.

Lola's voice coming from the front hit Sharon's body like the shock of a spear.

'I'm sorry, you'll have to forgive me, I'm nervous – I'm not really an up-the-front person. And I'm still quite new to all this. I mean, I don't know half as much as most of you sitting there – and I'm a mess myself, and my life's a muddle – I don't feel I've got a right to be up here, but I couldn't stay in my chair, I literally couldn't stay there, it was like my legs just walked themselves up here.'

The band played on, gentle chords picked out note by irritating note behind the skinny girl with the crazy hair and wide eyes.

Showy.

Sharon held her breath.

'I've got a picture in my head,' Lola's voice trembled on. 'It's a fruit bowl, and there's lots of beautiful fruit in there – but there's a lemon sitting at the bottom. And it's been there for a little while, and it's gone that sort of wrinkly, thin-skinned, hard way that lemons go after a few weeks. And – forgive me if this makes no sense – but I see a hand picking that lemon out, and putting it in a microwave – I know this sounds bonkers.' She paused, giggling lightly, breathily, manically.

Still Sharon held her breath. The girl sounded like a lunatic.

'Anyway, they put it in the microwave, this lemon, and when they get it out, it's all softened. And then they juice it, and there's loads of juice in the lemon, it just needed warming and rolling in the hands, and cutting open and squeezing. And it seems to me that it's a painful process, for a lemon to be heated and rolled and cut and squeezed. But through the pain, the lemon was brought to useful life.'

Lola stopped talking, and looked around her in blind panic. Sharon was pained at the memory of that feeling from a few years ago; that looking around the room wildly, not recognising a single face, not able to fix upon a single familiar feature.

'Thanks, Lola.' The pastor was up there now, his arm around Lola, his new favourite. He prayed the picture over the church.

Sharon let her breath out, long and heavy.

***

'That was interesting, wasn't it, Lola's word?' Jonathan said lightly, tipping the sherry into the cut crystal glasses. The cat paused between his ankles, looking up, waiting; hopeful.

'Not really,' is what it sounded like Sharon mumbled as she crushed peppercorns into the steak fillets on the cold marble slab before her.

Gemma, who'd come for lunch with Ruby, exchanged looks with Jonathan.

***

The next Sunday, Sharon watched Lola from the moment the service began. The girl was definitely sitting nearer the front this time, there was no doubt.

Sharon had claimed two seats in the back row for herself and Jonathan.

She watched the crazy hair from behind. Was it possible to have annoying hair? Yes, Sharon decided, it was, and Lola definitely had it. And the way she wore her coat was just plain old irritating. Showy, showy, *showy*.

During the worship, Sharon watched. When Lola's hands were raised, Sharon rolled her eyes. When Lola bowed during one song, Sharon tutted audibly. Jonathan took her hand, looked at her quizzically: she ignored him, hating him for his interest, sensing pity there, despising his ignorance: what a naïve man he was!

After the fourth song, Lola's upper body suddenly lurched forward so wildly that she might have hit the person in front of her. She raised her arms still higher, and the lurching continued. Within two minutes, she was on the stage.

'I'm up here again,' she said, and Sharon noticed the grin was less nervy, more...cocky. 'Once again, I haven't got any right to be up here. My life's a mess, like I told you last week. It's still a mess this week. It'll be a mess till the day I die, I guess. But anyway, I've had another picture, and I've had that thing with my legs again, like I had no choice about coming up here. My feet just brought me here.'

Sharon felt it: the pregnant pause in the room. The corporate holding of breath; waiting for wisdom. She saw Gemma sitting across the church, with Ruby on her lap, waiting to hear what was said, as if nothing at all was wrong.

'I've got a picture of the Statue of Liberty,' Lola said, and she laughed without any trace of fear at all. 'Yes, I know, it's another bonkers one. But what can I do? It ain't my idea!'

She actually paused for laughter then: *and it came.* Sharon clenched her fists.

'Anyway, there's this statue, standing in the harbour or wherever it is in New York – just like in all the movies you've ever seen. And it's got the crown-thing on, and it's holding its hand up, all triumphant. And the thing is, it's so *proud.* Like, it's got it all, this statue. It's saying, *look at me, look what I've done, look what I've got.* But, there's another part of this picture.'

The band played on, the music blending with the words. Sharon had to stand to get a better view of Lola.

'You see,' she went on, 'the statue is so... *hard.* It's made of metal, and it's so cold and hard. It's got this tough exterior, and it's looking out to sea, all proud and amazing looking – and it can do that, because it thinks that it's got the amazing city of New York behind it. But here's the other part of the picture.'

Sharon strained forward, trying to see better between all the heads in front of her. Jonathan placed an arm around her shoulders; she jerked it off, not looking at him, not wanting to see the hurt she knew she'd just caused.

'Coz there's nothing behind it. It's just on its own, looking out to sea, with sea behind it. It's got nothing to protect or proclaim. It's just a great big lump of metal, that's been made beautiful, out in the dark, swirly ocean. That's it.'

Lola's voice cracked, and everyone could see she was fighting back tears. The congregation strained forwards, all wishing her well and willing her to continue.

'That's it. If that's you, that's it. You've put yourself on some sort of pedestal, and you haven't looked to see if the thing that you're proclaiming is even still there – you're just a useless lump of metal in the ocean. And a big lump of metal in the middle of the sea is a hazard, not a symbol of celebration. And if that's you, you need to confess. I'm sorry saying that, it sounds really bad, I'm a bit weirded out saying that – sorry, if I'm mad, just ignore me.'

Lola was crying too much to speak now. She got down and returned to her seat. The pastor didn't come onto the stage. No one came onto the stage. The band played the same chords over and over, each musician searching the others' eyes for some signal that never came, looking around them for some direction as to their next step.

Still no one came onto the stage.

The band played on.

Sharon sank to her knees.

LET'S TALK

1. Which parts of this story particularly struck you?

   _____

   _____

   _____

2. In the first part of the story, Jonathan says to Sharon, '...as far as I can see it's entirely normal to never hear from God at all.' What do you think about that statement?

   _____

   _____

   _____

3. Sharon really struggles when Lola starts bringing her words and pictures to the congregation: could you empathise with Sharon in these feelings?

   _____

   _____

   _____

4. What do you do in order to hear from God?

   _____

   _____

   _____

   _____

5.	Have you had times when you've felt God has spoken to you loads, and times of apparent silence from heaven? What has helped you to 'tune back in' to God's voice?

_____

_____

_____

_____

6.	Are you ever tempted to put other Christians on some sort of holy pedestal?

_____

_____

_____

_____

7.	Have you ever had something you felt prompted to share with the church congregation, and not shared it? What held you back?

_____

_____

_____

_____

8.	What would you like Sharon to do after this story ends?

_____

_____

_____

_____

LET'S LISTEN

'You're blessed when you're at the end of your rope. With less of you there is more of God and his rule...

'You're blessed when you're content with just who you are – no more, no less...

'You're blessed when you've worked up a good appetite for God. He's food and drink in the best meal you'll ever eat.

'You're blessed when you care. At the moment of being 'care-full,' you find yourselves cared for.

'You're blessed when you get your inside world – your mind and heart – put right. Then you can see God in the outside world.'

Matthew 5: 3-9

'...You're here to be light, bringing out the God-colours in the world. God is not a secret to be kept. We're going public with this, as public as a city on a hill. If I make you light-bearers, you don't think I'm going to hide you under a bucket, do you? I'm putting you on a light stand. Now that I've put you there on a hilltop, on a light stand – shine! Keep open house; be generous with your lives. By opening up to others, you'll prompt people to open up with God, this generous Father in heaven.'

Matthew 5:14-16

'Simpletons! How long will you wallow in your ignorance? Cynics! How long will you feed your cynicism? Idiots! How long will you refuse to learn? About face! I can revise your life. Look, I'm ready to pour out my spirit on you; I'm ready to tell you all I know. As it is, I've called, but you've turned a deaf ear; I've reached out to you, but you've ignored me.'

Proverbs 1: 22-24

'But what happens when we live God's way? He brings gifts into our lives, much the same way that fruit appears in an orchard – things like affection for others, exuberance about life, serenity. We develop a willingness to stick with things, a sense of compassion in the heart, and a conviction that a basic holiness permeates things and people. We find ourselves involved in loyal commitments, not needing to force our way in life, able to marshal and direct our energies wisely.'

Galatians 5: 22-23

'Distress that drives us to God... turns us around. It gets us back in the way of salvation. We never regret that kind of pain. But those who let distress drive them away from God are full of regrets, end up on a deathbed of regrets.'

2 Corinthians 7:10

'Fear of God is a school in skilled living. First you learn humility, then you experience glory.'

Proverbs 15:33

'Pride lands you flat on your face; humility prepares you for honours.'

Proverbs 29:23

LET'S PRAY

Use this story as a launch pad for praying around any issues raised during your discussion time.

❖ Spend time specifically listening to God as a group: sit for two minutes in silence together (it may help to close your eyes), and give God space to speak. At the end of your time of silence, share any thoughts, words, pictures, scriptures or reminders that people sensed during that time.

PRAYER JOURNAL SPACE

_____

_____

_____

_____

_____

_____

_____

_____

_____

_____

_____

_____

_____

_____

_____

_____

_____

REFLECTIONS, LEARNING POINTS AND IDEAS FROM THIS SESSION...

WINNING

For Morris and Karen,
Christianity has become a competitive sport:
the question is, can they keep up?

K aren rushed across the church towards Morris with an expression that made him think something must have happened to one of their children

'Which one?' He sprang up, reaching out to her with both hands, ready for action.

'No, no, it's not the children. The children are fine.' Karen looked left and right and lowered her voice, leaning in closer to Morris. 'It's Anna and Richard,' she hissed. She pulled Morris away from the staring eyes around them and led him to an empty pew.

'What?' Morris said

Anna and Richard were their closest friends in the church. Confusion gave way to relief that the children were fine and then guilt at the realisation that he didn't really care about what happened to their friends. Morris rearranged his face to portray concern. 'What's happened? Are they hurt?'

'Hurt? Far from it. Oh,' Karen laughed without smiling, 'They've only gone and booked to go to Brazil, Morris! They're taking the kids to work with a project that helps street children, Morris! They've only gone and *done* it, Morris!'

Morris stepped back.

'They never mentioned going to book it up.'

'I know!' Not a word! And here we are, their *best* friends in church!'

'After all these years...' Morris sat down hard on the pew, and winced at the jarring in his back. 'All our talk about taking the kids overseas and giving them some real life faith lessons was, well, it was just, for me, it was just...'

'Talk?' Karen gripped his shoulder so tightly her fingernails turned white.

'I thought we were all just daydreaming together.'

'Me too! I never expected them to go ahead and actually do it. And now...' She sighed heavily and slumped down next to her husband.

'Now their kids are going to have missionary experience before they're even... how old are they?' Morris began to pull at his beard, scratching at an ingrowing hair on his jawline.

'Fourteen, eleven, ten, nine and seven.' Karen pulled at a wrinkle in her blouse.

'Same as ours. Right.'

'We've only got three, Morris.'

'Right. But same as our first three.' Morris said.

'We'll have to respond somehow.' Karen said.

'Yes, but how?'

The question hung in the air in the car all the way home from church. It lay heavy upon Morris and Karen at lunchtime, to the extent where – to the children's great relief – they forgot to make them eat all their vegetables and entirely neglected to grill them about their youth church sessions.

That afternoon, while their kids disappeared upstairs with mobile phones and the iPad, Morris and Karen got out all the Christian publications to which they subscribed and went on to the websites of every Christian charity they could think of. They compiled a list of potential responses to their friends' outstretched gauntlet.

1. Building an orphanage in Mozambique
2. Evangelising on a campus in Serbia and planting a new church there
3. Digging a well in Uganda
4. Building a toilet block in Papua New Guinea
5. Building dormitories for a school in Kenya
6. Assisting with an irrigation project in the Northern Territory in Australia
7. Supporting midwives in a clinic in Southern Sudan
8. Teaching at a Bible School in Ethiopia
9. Distributing food supplies in Bangladesh
10. Smuggling Bibles through China

They poured two large gin and tonics and sank down into their soft grey corner sofa to consider their options.

'Looks good, but was there nothing for Brazil?' Morris took a deep slurp.

'No, no, we can't go anywhere near Latin America, that's where *they're* going,' Karen said.

'Of course, sorry; silly me!' said Morris.

'I quite like the sound of the Northern Territory one.' Karen held her glass to the light, admiring the clear crystal that had been a wedding present eighteen years earlier.

'No one will think we're roughing it enough if we tell them we're going to Australia,' said Morris.

'You're quite right. Shame, though; I'd have loved to have pictures of the kids cuddling koalas,' said Karen.

'What about China?' Morris reached for an apple and crunched down on it.

'I don't want to actually *endanger* our children's lives simply for the sake of proving a point,' said Karen.

'No, of course not.' Morris pondered the list, turning the bite of apple over in his mouth with his tongue. 'Africa's so unstable.' His words were hard to distinguish through his mouthful.

'Yes, that's the problem with Africa. And Bangladesh – well, is there really any help for Bangladesh? With all that flooding? Would we be wasting our time?' said Karen.

'We want to build something that lasts,' Morris said.

'A legacy,' said Karen.

'Our children's legacy to the world,' said Morris, biting into the apple chunk that had grown warm in the pouch of his cheek.

'Mmm, what a lovely way to think of it.' Karen took a sip of the sharp, clear liquid and swallowed noisily. 'I remember a couple of years ago reading about a plane crash in Papua New Guinea. It's quite difficult terrain to navigate, if I remember rightly,' said Morris.

'That sounds a bit life-threatening. If you want to leave a legacy, you have to live at least long enough to get there, surely?' Karen raised an eyebrow.

'Very true. Suddenly this list is looking a bit sparse. Let's regroup and think it through again tomorrow evening,' said Morris.

'Sounds perfect – I think I'll take another one of these –' Karen lifted her glass, 'and have a bath. Can I get you one?'

'Why not?'

Morris crossed his legs, pushed back into the soft cushions of the sofa and reached for the remote control.

At 9:30 on Monday evening, Karen padded on stockinged feet down the hallway to the kitchen. The kids were finally settling down upstairs, and she was ready for her reward for a hard day's work. Morris, already leaning against the kitchen worktop, glass of red wine in hand, had clearly had the same idea.

She dimmed the lights, reached to undo the tortoise shell clip at the nape of her neck and ran her fingers roughly through her hair to loosen it.

'You're not going to believe this.' Karen took Morris's wine glass from the worktop and drank deeply, slowly, pacing her delivery, relishing the power of her fresh knowledge.

'What?' said Morris.

'It was the *kids* who wanted to go. *They* decided it *between themselves*.'

'What?' Morris grabbed his wine glass back fast. Karen took another glass from the kitchen cupboard and filled it too quickly, spilling Pinot Grigiot on the imitation granite worktop.

'Brazil. The Jones's.' she swiped at the spilt wine with a tea towel. 'Their kids decided they wanted to go between themselves. They've saved all their pay from all their part time jobs – paper rounds, gardening, babysitting, car washing – you name it, those kids are doing it.'

'No!' Morris refilled his glass.

'And, between them, they've raised the air fare for the entire family!'

'My God!' He gulped a mouthful down too fast and began coughing. Karen slapped his back.

'We haven't a hope!' said Karen.

'You're right.' Morris wiped at his watering eyes.

'I've tried to get our three excited about the idea of Sudan, but it's like they don't want to know,' Karen said.

'It's all over!' Morris said.

'James said he'd rather go back to the Lake District, he said there'd be no canoeing in the Sudan.'

'It's shameful!' Morris slapped a hand to his forehead.

'And Martha said that she wouldn't go anywhere without a McDonalds!'

'They might have one in Khartoum...' Morris said, making a mental note to *Google* it later.

'And Michael said he'd only go if we got him an Xbox and a stunt bike,' said Karen.

'Dear God.' Morris hung his head in his hands. 'It's hopeless! Our children are self-obsessed and materialistic and now they're making *us* look bad.'

'It's not like we haven't tried,' said Karen.

Morris looked into Karen's eyes, pleading, desperate; lost.

'All those bedtime prayers, all those bible studies... the repetition, the tedium, the constant drumming it all in... what's it all been for, Karen? I mean, *five kids fundraising to go on a mission trip*: how are we ever going to compete with that when our three are so selfish?'

Karen stood looking at him, trying to identify what she was feeling. Something was gnawing at the pit of her stomach. An unfamiliar sensation; perhaps a yearning, she thought. It felt a bit like hunger, or maybe sickness. And then she heard herself speaking, and it was almost as if this feeling in her belly was choosing the words.

'You know, Morris...' she said.

'Mmm?'

'We could just... let it go.'

'Let it go?' said Morris.

'Not *try* to go to Sudan. Go to the Lake District. Or Dorset. North Norfolk, maybe,' said Karen.

'Give up, you mean?' said Morris.

'Yes. Give up. Think how good it would feel not to try,' said Karen.

'I can't imagine it,' said Morris.

'I don't think I can keep going like this.' Karen found she was crying a little. 'It just makes me feel crap, and it makes me feel like our kids are awful.'

'I'm sorry Karen, but I really think that maybe they *are* awful.' Morris said.

'No! I'm sure they're not. They *can't* be. Not *our* kids. I agree, there's *loads* of awful kids at church, but not ours. I won't believe it of them. I went through three very painful labours to bring them into the world, Morris, and I need to feel that it was worth it.'

'They're the ones who won't raise the fare for Sudan!' Morris said.

'Listen to yourself!' Karen pulled at her hair and screwed her eyes tight shut. 'What's happened to us?'

'I'm not with you at all.' Morris frowned.

'Aren't you tired?' said Karen.

'Yes,' said Morris.

'Aren't you fed up with always feeling second rate?'

'Yes! God, yes.'

'Well, I just realised, Morris: we don't *have* to be tired *or* feel second rate.' Karen said.'

'But you said –'

'I know. I don't know where this thought's come from, Morris, except – well, maybe it's the Holy Spirit giving me a kick up the bum.'

'Does the Holy Spirit kick people up the bum?' Morris sighed, and stared into the bottom of his wine glass at the deep red dregs there. He closed his eyes and spoke quietly. 'It would be a big change, not trying anymore.'

'It would take time,' said Karen.

'I'd actually really enjoy not going to Sudan,' said Morris.

'I've always wanted to go canoeing on the river Dart,' said Karen.

'The kids would love that.' Morris smiled, just a little.

'It would be hard to tell Anna and Richard what we were doing,' said Karen.

'To admit that we'd failed,' said Morris.

'Perhaps we shouldn't give up so easily?' Karen opened the biscuit tin and began crunching a custard cream.

Morris stood up. 'Would we be admitting defeat?'

Karen pushed her finger around her back teeth, where the custard filling had gathered in the empty spaces once occupied by four fat, impacted wisdom teeth. 'I feel defeated.'

'Then perhaps we should,' said Morris.

'It would be lovely to admit feeling defeated.'

'You think so?' Morris reached into the biscuit tin, shuffled the contents around and emerged triumphant with a bourbon.

'To not pretend,' said Karen.

'Yes, I can see that.' Morris crunched his biscuit slowly. 'I could tell Richard we've come to realise our need to just rest in God's presence where we are.'

Karen caught his eye and something passed between them.

'To sow into our children's lives by... *family team-building?*'

They crunched their biscuits for a moment, before breaking into wide smiles. Morris started chuckling.

'That'll kill 'em!' he said, spraying bourbon crumbs everywhere.

Karen laughed so much she spilt the wine for a second time as she poured them each another glass. They raised their drinks in a toast to their genius.

She had that funny feeling in her belly again. She couldn't put a finger on it. That unreachable, un-nameable sense of something – something – *something...*She pushed it aside.

LET'S TALK

1. What stood out in this story for you?

    _____

    _____

    _____

    _____

2. Why do you think Morris and Karen feel threatened by their friends' decision to go to Brazil?

    _____

    _____

    _____

    _____

3. What did you think of the way Morris and Karen considered their options for going overseas?

    _____

    _____

    _____

    _____

4. Have you ever experienced competitiveness between Christians? Did the story ring true for you in any way?

    _____

    _____

    _____

    _____

5. If you could sit down and have a chat with Karen and Morris, what would you say to each of them?

    _____

    _____

    _____

6. Are you ever tempted to put a spin on your actions to make them sound more 'worthy' to other Christians?

    _____

    _____

    _____

7. In what ways are you tempted to 'compete' with other Christians?

    _____

    _____

    _____

8. Do you think Morris and Karen will ever feel contented?

    _____

    _____

    _____

9. If we are to approach God as children, what does this really entail? Think about the children featured in this story; how do they lay out their desires? What do you think about this?

    _____

    _____

    _____

LET'S LISTEN

'Don't look for shortcuts to God. The market is flooded with sure-fire, easy-going formulas for a successful life that can be practiced in your spare time. Don't fall for that stuff, even though crowds of people do. The way to life – to God! – is vigorous and requires total attention.'

Matthew 7:13-14

'There's trouble ahead when you live only for the approval of others, saying what flatters them, doing what indulges them. Popularity contests are not truth contests – look how many scoundrel preachers were approved by your ancestors! Your task is to be true, not popular.'

Luke 6:26

'...every church will know that appearances don't impress me. I x-ray every motive...'

Revelation 2:23

'Be especially careful when you are trying to be good so that you don't make a performance out of it. It might be good theatre, but the God who made you won't be applauding.'

Matthew 6:1

'You're blessed when you can show people how to cooperate instead of compete or fight. That's when you discover who you really are, and your place in God's family.'

Matthew 5:9

'These children are the kingdom's pride and joy. Mark this: Unless you accept God's kingdom in the simplicity of a child, you'll never get in.'

Luke 18: 17

LET'S PRAY

Use the story as a launch pad for prayer with and for one another.

❖ Pray that God would guard your hearts against wrong motivation.

❖ Pray that there wouldn't be any spirit of competitiveness amongst Christians in your church family, but that instead there would be support, encouragement and mutual building up in Christ.

❖ If you ever feel guilty for simply doing something you enjoy for the sake of enjoying it, give this up to God.

PRAYER JOURNAL SPACE

_____

_____

_____

_____

_____

_____

_____

_____

_____

_____

_____

_____

_____

_____

_____

_____

REFLECTIONS, LEARNING POINTS AND IDEAS FROM THIS SESSION...

FACE PAINTING

Willow is struggling with loneliness in church:
tough when you're the vicar's wife.

The small, muddy rectangle in the middle of the Churchill Estate was crawling with Christians. This patch of brown was bordered by a four-storey yellow-brick block of flats on each side. Residents from Winston House, Victory House, Dunkirk House and Black Dog House watched through tightly shut windows, hidden behind the safety of net curtains.

Phone calls had been passing between the flats for the last hour.

'You going out there, Bill?'

'Not if I can help it. I'll check the windows again when Countdown's finished.'

'I can't concentrate on Countdown, not with that racket going on out there...'

Down below, the hired bouncy castle lurched wildly, dangerously overloaded with the boisterous offspring of the congregation who were giving it a serious pounding. Two teenage members of the church's youth group were supervising, their phones held vigilantly aloft, capturing images of screaming, colliding children and diligently posting them across a variety of internet platforms.

Willow shifted in her seat, her bottom in the final throes of pain before going numb from the cold plastic of the old garden chair she had been stationed on for the last hour and a half. Sitting before her, swinging his little legs, was a perfect Spiderman.

'There you go, all done,' Willow forced a smile and leaned back, rolling her shoulders slowly, stiffly. She put the face-painting brush into the water pot, which looked like a jar of black ink with a swirl of glitter floating on the top. Spiderman continued to sit there, legs swinging, face frozen.

'You're done, love, you can go now.'

Still, he didn't hear her. Willow touched his knee, and the child jumped in fright.

'You're done. Go and play, Spiderman.'

As the tiny superhero slipped silently away, the next child, fresh-faced and beautiful, took his place.

'Who do you want to be?' Willow asked, taking the brush back out of the dirty water and wiping it on a fresh piece of kitchen paper, pulling at the bristles in an attempt to draw the last of the black-red make-up out.

'Spiderman,' the boy said.

Willow smiled through a sigh, and pushed the brush's sticky bristles into the thick red paint.

Face painting whilst keeping an eye on her own three kids was proving as impossible as she'd suspected it would be.

As she daubed the child's forehead, she saw her husband pass by. Despite being just a few feet away, David did not see Willow. He was in full vicar-mode; smiling in a general way, murmuring vague hellos to the teenagers whose names, Willow knew, he could never remember.

Something tightened in Willow's chest as she watched him. He looked endearingly sweet; happy, hopeful. He paused at the refreshment stall just next to the face painting. Willow wished he would see her, but he'd gone past now, and Mary Crouch, who'd been complaining loudly for the last hour, had got hold of David's arm.

'I mean, David,' Mary gushed, 'how can we possibly guarantee a *nut-free* church? It's not possible, David, it's not! I can't monitor and regulate to that extent – I've already taken on far more than I can –'

'Let's talk about this in the week, Mary.' David was doing The Smile, that one he did these days that had nothing to do with the rest of his face or his body; pure muscle control and an exercise in stamina. 'I'll get Sheila to check my diary and fix a time to talk about it.'

Willow dipped the little brush into the dirty water, wiped it off and dragged it through the black face paint.

David had moved on. Mary Crouch was still muttering something.

Willow closed her eyes for a second, then re-focussed on the little face before her and began, again, to paint.

She needed to talk to David, too, about everything. Perhaps, she thought, her eyebrow arching, she should get Sheila to book her an appointment to see David, like everybody else.

Last night's confrontation still whirled around and around in her head like the glitter swirling in the inky blackness of the paintbrush pot.

'Trevor Gordon's niece works in Starbucks in town.' David's face had been cold, somehow flat; his emotions impossible to read. 'She's seen you there every Sunday morning between eleven and twelve for the last two months.'

Willow had looked at the floor; said nothing. Like a teenager, she thought, with David playing the role of Angry Parent. They'd stood frozen in the kitchen, the silence heavy between them.

In the lounge, there were eight house group leaders waiting for their meeting to start. Willow wanted to have this conversation so much, but not now, not with people in the house. And the house was always so full of people! She cringed just thinking about how David had taken hold of her arms and squeezed them, and given her The Smile.

'I understand – I really do.'

He'd pulled her into an embrace and she'd held her hands – wet and foamy from the washing up – away from his clean, black shirt. She could feel his dog collar pushing against her cheekbone. He spoke softly, his mouth by her ear.

'If it makes you happy, then fine. All I ask of you is that you return for the end of the service and smile at a few people over coffee. It doesn't even have to be a real smile – you're always saying you miss the acting profession – well, here's your chance! That way, those who stayed in church will think you were in the crèche, and those who were in crèche will think you were in church.'

Willow had pulled back, her eyes roaming across David's face, searching, yearning for some trace of the twinkle that would confirm this as a joke.

'You've actually thought this all through, haven't you?' She stared at him.

'It would be very discouraging to others in the congregation to hear that the vicar's wife doesn't like going to church, wouldn't it?'

'Yes,' she heard herself say.

'And you don't want to discourage the congregation, do you?'

'Of course not.'

'Well then.'

He'd turned and gone into the lounge with his plate of Hobnobs as if all was resolved.

'That hurts.' The child in front of Willow was squirming, and she realised she'd been pushing the brush hard into the corner of his mouth, oblivious to the present.

'I'm so sorry, love.' She stopped and touched his face. 'I didn't mean to hurt you.'

She dipped the brush back into the water pot.

'You're all done, now. Go and have some fun.' She forced a smile. A new child sat in the seat and said 'Spiderman,' before she'd even asked the question.

She looked along the line of children, which hadn't shortened for the hour since she'd set up the two chairs, and put the face paints out on a little camping step. The queue seemed to mutate and re-form, like amoeba splitting, Willow thought. Boden-clad, gappy-toothed, floppy-haired amoeba; a beautiful bunch of Ezekials, Kezias, Esthers, Micahs and Ahimelechs. Well, okay, maybe there weren't any Ahimelechs. (So many times Willow had been tempted to introduce her eldest, Saffy, as 'Jezebel' or 'Bathsheba,' in Christian circles, just to see what would happen next).

David was standing at the church sign-up stall; he must've walked past her again without seeing her.

Willow watched him, feeling that she was watching The Church in action. He was still smiling. She saw his eyes following the Gordons, the Smiths and Dear Old Betty Long. He had the face of a proud parent, beaming at what he had created. The shine soon went out of his eyes at the sound of Sheila Patterson's voice. David's secretary was half his size but spoke with all the volume and certainty of a tank commander heading into battle.

David was saying something to her, smiling eagerly, like a child trying to impress a teacher. It wasn't working.

'A single circuit of this event has convinced me of the need to run a parenting course as quickly as possible in the church,' she boomed, insistent that all around should hear her thoughts.

David squirmed visibly, tried to start laughing and began looking around desperately. It was at this moment that his eye finally came to rest on Willow. He looked surprised, then relieved to see her, and she knew that he'd already assumed she wasn't there, that she'd taken herself off to Starbucks once again.

Sheila was still shouting. 'Did *you* invite anyone, David?'

David pulled at his hair, shrugged his shoulders, held out his hands, tried to say something.

'Well, I don't know anyone from the estate,' Sheila boomed on, 'so I can hardly be blamed for the appalling turn-out.'

David's face fell, and Willow felt a revulsion for Sheila, and a surprising defensive pang for her husband; she wished she could reach out to him, somehow.

A cry from the bouncy castle demanded attention, and Sheila stomped off in that direction.

Willow watched David stepping slowly backwards, behind the sign-up stall. When he was out of the way of bags and boxes of Alpha leaflets, he turned and walked to their car, got in and drove off.

Willow blinked, and then focussed on the boy's red and black face.

'Am I done, then?' the child before her asked.

'Yes,' she'd entirely forgotten he was there, and was surprised to see she had replicated a perfect Spiderman's face without any conscious thought.

She turned back to look for David and the car, but he had gone.

A soft, Scottish accent interrupted her thoughts.

'Excuse me, love, but I've just found this lad down the road there, and he says you're his mum.'

Willow looked up and saw a woman in her fifties, softly chubby with pearly pink lipstick and powdered cheeks, holding her youngest son's hand.

'Oh, Finn, not again!'

'Don't be cross with him.' The woman smiled, 'There's no harm done. Look, why don't you paint his face? You can't sit here all day and not paint your own son's face.'

'He won't sit still long enough.' Willow smiled back at the woman.

'He'll sit on my lap.'

The woman planted herself on the plastic chair in front of Willow and heaved Finn onto her lap, wrapping her big arms around his little tummy to form a human seatbelt, holding him securely in place. She seemed not to hear the tuts, groans and murmurings of 'Not fair!' coming from the queue. She spoke brightly to Finn, as if nothing was wrong.

'What are you going to be, son? A pirate?' She looked around for inspiration. 'Spiderman?' She caught Willow's eye and laughed. 'I'm Eleanor,' she said, 'folks call me Ellie.'

Willow laughed back, feeling a concertina of creases on her forehead unfolding.

'I'm Willow. Pleased to meet you.' She noticed that she really felt it, too. She smiled at Finn with a new sense, the thrill of a secret joke shared.

'What shall I paint you as, Finn? Who will you be?'

'Just me,' said Finn.

'Don't be crazy, you can't just be you.' Willow giggled. 'You need to choose someone else to be.'

'But I just want to be me,' Finn said looking as if he might cry.

'Good for you.' Eleanor gave him a squeeze and then, suddenly, she peered very closely at Willow's face in the way that many strangers had in the last decade. Willow was used to it now, and waited for the inevitable question. 'Don't I know you from somewhere?'

Willow smiled and braced herself for potential embarrassment. 'Possibly.'

'You famous?'

'I was in an advert, about ten years ago. A silly advert that I thought was my Big Break.'

'What was it for?' Eleanor was still examining Willow's face in the way people seemed to feel free to; it used to make Willow uncomfortable years ago, but she'd got used to the experience with time. Sort of.

'It was for home insurance. I lived in my dream house, only it all fell down around me.'

'I remember!' Eleanor bounced with a flash of excitement, making Finn laugh at the unexpected jiggling he received. 'The ceiling plaster fell off and the water was up to your knees and then, right at the end, a –'

'A dinosaur stood on mummy's roof!' Finn chipped in, enjoying the chance to deliver the punch line.

Eleanor clapped her hands. 'Have you watched mummy on the telly?'

'Mummy showed us on YouTube.' Finn beamed with pride.

'That advert used to make me laugh.' Eleanor wiggled Finn from side to side, making him chuckle. 'It was the expression on your mum's face that was so funny. I can still remember the slogan –'

Willow joined her and they spoke the words in perfect unison: 'For whatever life throws at you!'

'So, does your mummy still act?' Eleanor asked Finn.

Willow threw her head back and laughed. 'Bless you for calling that acting!' She wiped a tear from her eye and sighed. 'I haven't done anything for years. I've got three kids, a husband who's at the beck and call of pretty much everyone else except me, and I haven't worked out how to fit anything I'd like to do in yet.' Willow's smile disappeared.

'Where are your other two?'

'Saffy's on the bouncy castle, and Jonas is the one causing all the fuss in the ball pool. Finn you've already met.'

'And what a lovely boy he is, too.' Eleanor jiggled her knees up and down, making Finn giggle. 'I'm so glad to have met you, young man.'

Finn blushed and doubled over, still giggling, squeezing the insides of his knees tight against his hot face. Eleanor looked at the queue of children and back at Willow.

'So, if you're painting faces, how are you keeping your eyes on your own kids?'

'Very badly,' said Willow, feeling the tears welling. She blinked, trying to beat the waters back with her eyelids.

'Come with me,' Eleanor stood, nudging Finn off her lap. 'Come on –' she reached out her hand to Willow.

Willow looked down the long line of grumpy children.

'Come on,' Eleanor said again. 'Life's too short to paint faces. Come to my flat. I've got a nice fruitcake, and the kids can watch a video.'

'I –'

'This isn't you, is it? Not at the moment.'

'How did you –?'

'I'm right, aren't I?'

Willow looked back at the row of children. Eleanor waited, hand held out.

'I only live in that block there – Dunkirk House. Come and have something to eat with me, and take a break.'

'Let me get Saffy and Jonas.' Willow stood, placing the brush flat by the paints.

'What do you think you're doing?' Sheila's voice boomed across the queue. 'You're supposed to be painting faces.'

'I need a break,' Willow replied. 'Perhaps you could man the stall for me for twenty minutes?'

Willow heard the tuts of protest Sheila made behind her as Eleanor pulled her away. She caught sight of David pulling up in the car just as she squeezed Saffy's foot into its shoe.

'Where are you off to?' he called, his voice tight, a pile of parish magazines in his hands.

'I'm going for a cup of tea with a lady I've just met,' Willow said, and she turned to indicate her new friend. 'This is Ellie.'

'Willow!' David lurched forward and grabbed hold of her arm.

'I'll just be over here looking for Saffy's other shoe,' Eleanor said.

'Willow, you can't just go off! You're on the Welcome Committee! You can't...' the light on his face changed, and he began to smile. 'Oh, unless... yes, I see what you're doing! Good luck! Listen, though –' He leaned in conspiratorially. 'I'd better warn you: I recognise this lady, and she's a tough nut to crack! The last curate had his head bitten off by her over something or other. Probably best to filter her into the 9:15 communion crowd. Yes! That's the thing to invite her to. Good luck, Willow!'

'But I'm not planning on inviting her to church,' Willow said, 'I'm only going to have a cup of tea and five minutes peace.'

Anxiety wrinkled David's brow once more.

'We're not here just to have a cup of tea and a chat, Willow! We're supposed to be *witnessing*, and you're supposed to be painting faces!'

'You're witnessing right now, David,' Willow hissed, horribly aware of the stares they were attracting from the church family.

'I –' David's shoulders drooped. He looked around him and back at Willow.

Willow stared at him, silent; praying.

'Willow, I-'

'I'm going with Ellie for a cup of tea. When I get back, we need to talk. About everything.'

'Yes.'

He was looking at her like a child; a six-foot-tall Finn, lost and alone and worried that no one was looking for him.

'We'll talk,' she said, gently.

'David?' Sheila's voice sliced through the moment. David didn't answer. Willow searched his eyes urgently with her own. She sighed.

'There's too many people here, David. I just need a little bit of space from all these people. They're exhausting me.'

'I know.' David wiped at his eyes with his sleeve.

'David?' Sheila's voice was louder this time.

He leaned forward and took Willow in his arms; parish magazines fell all over the muddy ground around them.

'I wish I could come with you,' he whispered in her ear.

'David!' Sheila sounded furious.

'Yes, Sheila,' he said, fighting with his facial muscles to pull The Smile back into action.

Willow turned and stepped towards Eleanor. She felt a hand on her shoulder; David's hand.

'I really *do* want to talk, Willow.'

'When I get back,' Willow made sure everyone saw her smiling at David, and then she headed towards Eleanor, who had gathered Saffy, Jonas and Finn under her arms like chicks.

LET'S TALK

1. What stood out in this story for you?

    _____

    _____

    _____

    _____

2. What would you like to say to Willow, David and Sheila about the
    roles they are each playing in this story?

    _____

    _____

    _____

    _____

    _____

    _____

    _____

    _____

    _____

3. How would you like to see things change for Willow and David?

    _____

    _____

    _____

    _____

4. Do you think the way Willow's feeling is unusual?

_____

_____

_____

_____

5. Have you ever experienced loneliness in church? How have you dealt with it?

_____

_____

_____

_____

6. Has God ever reached out to you in ways you didn't expect?

_____

_____

_____

_____

LET'S LISTEN

'Are you tired? Worn out? Burned out on religion? Come to me. Get away with me and you'll recover your life. I'll show you how to take a real rest. Walk with me and work with me – watch how I do it. Learn the unforced rhythms of grace. I won't lay anything heavy or ill-fitting on you. Keep company with me and you'll learn to live freely and lightly.'

Matthew 11: 28-30

'Look at me. I stand at the door. I knock. If you hear me call and open the door, I'll come right in and sit down to supper with you...'

Revelation 3:20

'...Come off by yourselves; let's take a break and get a little rest...'

Mark 6:31-32

'Here's what I want you to do: Find a quiet, secluded place so you won't be tempted to role-play before God. Just be there as simply and honestly as you can manage. The focus will shift from you to God, and you will begin to sense his grace.'

Matthew 6:6

LET'S PRAY

Use the discussion you've had as a launch pad for prayer for each other, and for anyone feeling lonely within the church.

❖ Give thanks for the people who've been friendly towards you.

❖ Thank God that he never forgets you, but always reaches out to you.

PRAYER JOURNAL SPACE

REFLECTIONS, LEARNING POINTS AND IDEAS FROM THIS SESSION...

FAMILIAR STRANGERS

*Travis is thrilled to be invited to David and Sarah's wedding – until
some guests there bring back memories of church experiences
that he's still struggling to make sense of.*

Travis was surprised to be invited to David and Sarah's wedding. He'd
known them both, a little, during his time at the Baptist church, but that
was four churches ago. He'd been in a home group with Sarah and, while
he'd liked her very much, they hadn't exactly socialised together. It was
more than two years since he'd seen either of them; two years in which
Travis had accumulated acquaintances and familiar strangers at the URC,
St. Mary's, Vineyard and, most recently, Bloomfield NFI, where he hadn't
been for the last three Sundays.

Having had no reason to say no – no prior engagement, no demanding
relatives of his own seeking to monopolise his weekend – Travis had
accepted David and Sarah's invitation. As he'd dropped his reply in to the
post box outside the grey block of flats where he lived, he'd felt that first
twinge of anxiety over the prospect of being reunited with a group of
people he hadn't kept in touch with, and who, he was suddenly aware,
might feel he had chosen to deliberately remove himself from.

It hadn't felt like that at the time of leaving the Baptist church, but he
could see that it may have appeared that way, and he knew that trying to
explain would only make it seem more like he was making excuses. Better
to say nothing.

In the church, he'd slipped into the back row, with the work colleagues
and neighbours, and those from the Baptist congregation who hadn't
actually been invited but who stood by the principle that a wedding is a
public occasion and were jolly well going to be attending on that basis.

Across the church, Travis could see several familiar heads and backs: the stooped shoulders of Minnie Hedges; the stiff, straight spine of Brian Kew; the enormous, wild frizzy hair of Shana Taylor; the neat, short grey bristly head of Colin Green. There were many he recognised but couldn't name. A room full of familiar strangers. But then, church had always felt that way to Travis.

As his eyes roamed the backs, the suits, the hats, those crazy little feathery things women wore on their heads these days, he began to recognise the backs of other familiar strangers from other churches. Those large, round shoulders certainly matched his memory of Lucia Bryson, and the slight bony figure beside her was definitely Gordon, her nervy husband. Travis tried to recall which church they were from – for a moment he was stuck. It was either the URC or St Mary's... In the end he pinned them to St Mary's, a mental image forming of them side by side in the hatch opening at the back of the church, serving teas and coffees after the service.

Looking across to the left aisle, Travis spotted someone from Vineyard, a young woman with bright turquoise hair and a matching turquoise nose stud; he'd always been slightly nervous of her. She was sitting with her arm around a large man with red hair who looked like... yes, it was, Travis was sure, it was Tom from Bloomsfield NFI! Travis had been in a small group at Bloomsfield with Tom for a while, he'd liked him. He'd forgotten all about him until just now.

The first few bars of a recent pop song suddenly flooded the sound system, and everybody around Travis stood. His legs straightened on autopilot, so that he was standing with everyone else just in time to see Sarah enter the church on her father's arm. She looked nervous and beautiful.

Travis had reached the grand old age of twenty-nine without meeting The One. There had been romances, but no one yet had caused him to lose sleep with yearning or stopped him from concentrating on his research in the university library. He'd met plenty of girls during the two degrees he'd undertaken at Bloomsfield University, less since he'd begun his masters in philosophy. Even less who understood his faith or who had any sort of faith of their own.

Travis had arrived in Bloomsfield eight years ago, freshly orphaned, having inherited a house in London from his mother (who'd died suddenly, unexpectedly so that Travis would never recover from the shock of losing her). Before Bloomsfield, he'd been drifting through life, working in shops and cafes, wondering where it was all leading. After his mother's passing, he'd found tenants for the house and hurled himself in a different direction: university. He chose Bloomsfield because it was a small university in a small city.

In fresher's week he'd met Clarrie, who'd invited him to an Alpha course that was running at All Souls. The course had been a revelation, a lightbulb moment for Travis. Suddenly existence had meaning and direction, and he'd surrendered his life to Christ with a huge sense of relief. But then Clarrie had got a job in Holland and moved away. Without any other connections, Travis had slowly slipped away from All Souls, his attendance dwindling almost imperceptibly to the members of the church, so that one week someone leaned over to their friend before the service and said 'I haven't seen that young man with the long hair for a while,' and her friend replied, 'Long hair? I can't think who you mean,' and there he was, or rather, wasn't.

Travis had slipped out of the C of E and into the back row of the Methodists, where he'd met Angie. It had taken six turbulent months to admit to themselves that they were a terrible combination. After the row-to-end-all-rows, they'd finally called it a day. With Angie being the minister's daughter, it had always been clear which one of them would be leaving the church if things didn't work out.

For a long time, Travis hadn't gone to any church. The relationship with Angie had rather confused things and put him off the idea of church altogether. He nursed his wounds in the college library, and nurtured his faith quietly and privately, with books and podcasts.

It was not long after that that Travis had found his way into the Baptists. They offered tea and toast at three o'clock on Saturday mornings to students at the end of a long night out. Travis had never been into pubs or clubs, but he frequently worked through the night at the University's twenty-four hour library, just a short walk from the Baptist church. The lure of being cooked for, even if it was only buttered toast, was irresistible. David had been there the first time he'd gone, buttering toast, and they'd got chatting. Travis wondered if David still did the tea and toast thing. He would ask him at the reception: that would give him something to say.

David was holding Sarah's hand now, grinning widely at his bride as the band began to play the first hymn.

It was during this hymn that Travis spotted Angie halfway down the right hand aisle. Panic seized his gut so that he leaned suddenly forward, his hand to where the jab of pain had stabbed at his belly like a knife: how on earth did Sarah know Angie? Dread flooded his veins like the icy chill of anaesthetic. Angie, who he now referred to privately as Angry Angie, had scared the life out of Travis with a possessive streak that needed to pin him down, force him to commit, sign him up for things... his resistance had hit all her insecurity buttons and convinced her that he must be seeing other girls, that he couldn't be trusted, that he didn't care - that he was of dubious character.

She hadn't seen him yet, he was sure of it. Gradually, Travis's heart rate returned to normal, and the panic in his mind began to clear like mist rising.

During the sermon, Travis began to reflect on the mistakes he'd made in his relationship with Angie for the millionth time; about the things he wished he'd done differently. Her hair looked lovely today: she'd somehow entwined wildflowers, tiny and delicate, into a thick plait. The thin ribbon straps of her dress reminded him that her neck flowed like liquid being poured into the fine vessel of her body. Her shoulders were angular; strong but fine-boned. Stubborn, rigid, passionate. The few years since he'd seen her had been the ones where she had changed from a self-conscious teenage girl to a beautiful young woman. She must have been away to university and come back herself, by now.

As if sensing his gaze, Angie turned and stared directly at Travis. He dropped his head and stared at his lap as soon as she looked - but he caught enough to know that she was surprised to see him here, and that she was horrified by his presence. She wriggled her shoulders as if trying to shake something off, and then lifted one slender, bare arm and wrapped it around a young man sitting to her left. She glanced back at Travis one more time - a warning shot? A gloat? - Travis couldn't be sure of her meaning. He only knew it wasn't joy at seeing him.

He shifted his gaze elsewhere, over the rows directly in front of him. His heart rate was rising again, sharply. He could hear the blood pumping in his ears, and then he spotted Ross, one of the elders at Bloomsfield NFI.

Two months ago, Ross had sat in Travis's kitchen and gone through a membership form. Travis had wanted to help out with the P.A. team at church, but he had been terrified to discover that, in order to do so, he must become a member of the church officially. As Ross had sat there and spoken of long-term commitment and dependability, his voice had somehow merged in Travis's head with Angie's constant demands, and the dread of those days had returned. Travis hadn't felt able to sign anything right away, but had asked for time to think it over. One of the questions Ross had asked was why he'd left any previous churches he'd been to, and Travis had suddenly felt ashamed at what was clearly a catalogue of failures – failure to connect, to knit in, to commit... Ross had used the word 'church hopper' – but he wasn't church hopping, was he? He just hadn't found the right one, yet. And it was the same God in all of them, right?

During the last hymn and the blessing, Travis felt his cheeks growing hot. Soon the service would be over, and Ross would stand up and turn around and see him and know that he hadn't been to church for three weeks and that he definitely was a church hopper and not someone worth investing in long-term.

Travis began to feel the heat prickle at the skin beneath his shirt collar. He pulled at his tie and stretched his chin upwards. At least he was in the back row, nice and near the exit. He could slip out easily, and then there was just the reception to get through.

He escaped silently in the last verse of the last hymn while all eyes were on the happy couple, and made his way to the church hall where the reception was being hosted. A thought had occurred to him, and he needed to check something rather urgently.

The doors to the hall were unlocked, and, inside, the catering staff were carrying plates and bowls for the buffet, setting out wine bottles and giving napkins a final straightening.

The seating plan was on a board on a large easel in the entrance area. Travis scanned the tables for his name. He found it under a list called 'Great Expectations,' which threw him momentarily until he saw that the other tables were called 'Pride and Prejudice,' 'Wuthering Heights,' 'Jamaica Inn,' and 'Middlemarch,' and remembered that Sarah and David were both English teachers. He scanned the names surrounding his on the list, and his greatest fears were confirmed.

The obvious and, for Travis, natural course of action was set. He slipped out of the hall just in time to see Sarah and David coming out of the church doors. Sarah saw him and beamed, reaching out for him.

'Travis!'

Drawn in irresistibly to the beautiful bride, he put an arm around her waist and shook David's hand at the same time.

'Congratulations.' He smiled. He really did like Sarah and David. He couldn't think now why he'd left the Baptist church. There hadn't really been anything wrong with it. Perhaps it was worth a second try...

The photographer was letting the guests mill around freely in the churchyard, snapping away. He took a picture of Travis with Sarah and David, all three looking hopeful.

Moments later, Travis weaved quietly through the crowd of well-wishers, taking a sharp left at the sight of Angie, a quick right when he spotted Ross ahead of him, and bending to do his shoe and hide his head at the sight of the girl with the turquoise hair. By the time he'd made it through the crowd, people were heading towards the church hall for the reception. No one was looking at Travis, and he was pretty confident that no one saw him slip away.

LET'S TALK

1. What struck you most about Travis' story?

    _____

    _____

    _____

    _____

    _____

2. '...There were many he recognised but couldn't name. A room full of familiar strangers. But then, church had always felt that way to Travis.' Can you relate to the way Travis is feeling at this point in the story?

    _____

    _____

    _____

    _____

    _____

3. 'He wasn't church hopping, was he? He just hadn't found the right one, yet. And it was the same God in all of them, right?' How would you respond to Travis at this moment of his thinking?

    _____

    _____

    _____

    _____

    _____

4. 'He scanned the names surrounding his on the list, and his greatest fears were confirmed.' Who else do you think was on Travis's table at the wedding reception? What do you think Travis's greatest fears are?

_____

_____

_____

_____

5. If you were at Sarah and David's wedding, and had the opportunity to speak with Travis, what would you want to ask him or tell him?

_____

_____

_____

_____

6. Do you think it's a good idea to commit to one congregation, or should there be more freedom of movement between churches?

_____

_____

_____

_____

LET'S LISTEN

'Let me give you a new command: love one another. In the same way I loved you, you love one another. This is how everyone will recognise that you are my disciples – when they see the love you have for each other.'

John 13:34-35

'If you enter a place of worship and, about to make an offering, you suddenly remember a grudge a friend has against you, abandon your offering, leave immediately, go to this friend and make things right. Then and only then, come back and work things out with God.'

Matthew 5:23-24

'...the time is coming – it has, in fact, come – when what you're called will not matter and where you go to worship will not matter.
'It's who you are and the way you live that count before God. Your worship must engage your spirit in the pursuit of truth. That's the kind of people the Father is out looking for: those who are simply and honestly themselves before him in their worship. God is sheer being itself – Spirit. Those who worship him must do it out of their very being, their spirits, their true selves, in adoration.'

John 4: 23-24

LET'S PRAY

Pray around any issues that have come out of this evening's discussion.

❖ Pray that we shall, as Christians, indeed be recognised by the love we have for each other.

❖ Pray for those who feel rootless, that they will find the family God has for them.

PRAYER JOURNAL SPACE

REFLECTIONS, LEARNING POINTS AND IDEAS FROM THIS SESSION...

HOUSE GROUP LEADER ON THE EDGE

Peter deals with the challenges of leadership in his own way.

At times of stress, Peter turns his life into poetry. Limericks, to be precise. Limericks which he speaks aloud in surprisingly good impressions of celebrities' voices, to be even more precise.

He's been doing it since he was fourteen. He's forty-two now, so he'll probably be doing it 'til the day he dies. It enables him to give vent to his frustrations in a structured format, and there are many frustrations in Peter's life. Somehow, in those five lines he feels safe and satisfied with a sense of pressure released. He only ever recites poetry aloud at home, or when alone somewhere. At work – in front of a class of teenage boys who need to pass their GCSE and A level Physics exams – well, it wouldn't be helpful.

As we join Peter, we find him in his kitchen, leaning over a blackened frying pan on the stove top before him and checking his cheese omelette's progress (nicely browning and pleasingly oozy). The tentative sunshine of a spring evening reaches its thin fingers through the window over the sink and lays its cautious warmth on Peter's shoulder and he is grateful for it. It was light when he got in from work this evening for the first time in months. In the pale rays he feels some hope: change will come. He turns to his phone to check over the words of the text he has just composed.

Hi there! House group at mine this week. Let me know if you're coming?!

Questing yet jovial, he thinks to himself; the tone is probably about right for a house group leader, which is just what our Peter is.

He checks once more that he's included each of the members of his group in the message address list, presses 'send', and watches his phone until it confirms that his text has made its way successfully to its ten intended recipients.

Peter speaks aloud as the text ding-dongs its successfully-sent status, his voice a perfect replication of English actor, Brian Blessed.

'A house group leader from Leicester
Sent texts to his house group to pester
Will you come? Said the fool
Who'd forgotten that all
Of his house-group ignored his requesters...'

An acrid smell hits Peter's nostrils and he speaks again as he scrapes his pan, splatting the last of the burned egg onto a plate and covering it all in brown sauce. His voice now mimics Prince Charles' ponderous tones perfectly.

'My poor omelette's dead as a doornail,
The cheese is as dry as a hay bale.
My food looks so bad
That to eat it's too sad
I would much rather chew on a toenail.'

He puts the plate on an old tin tray and carries it through to the lounge, where he switches the TV onto something mindless about couples who want big houses in the countryside, far away from people. The sofa creaks alarmingly as he sits down, and he feels a spring pushing into his bottom through the sagging brown leather.

The burnt eggy-cheesy mix is barely scratching the insides of his throat when three rapid rings of his doorbell demand his attention. He sighs, plonks his tray onto the empty side of the sofa and heaves himself to standing.

'Did you get a chance to look through the paperwork yet?' Peter's neighbour, Jean, sways on his doorstep. The swaying is beginning to get on Peter's nerves; he watches her - left, right, left, right - she always stands as if she is holding a baby, or hearing music.

'I'm sorry, Jean, I haven't had a moment yet - I've had parents' evenings so far this week.'

'I really need to know about it, Peter, I mean, if I've got a shortfall I'll need to make it up, won't I? I don't want to pass on a debt in my will, do I? I don't think my daughters would thank me for that, would they? I should say not!'

Jean beams and Peter wonders whether to suggest her daughters might consider helping her with her paperwork.

Instead, he forces a smile.

'Yes, Jean,' he says, 'I'll try and have a look at it tonight.'

He thinks about how having a neighbour who goes to the same church as him is a mixed blessing.

The phone rings, liberating him from Jean's fixed grin and piercing eyes.

'I must answer that,' he says, shutting the door. He can still see Jean swaying through the glass as he begins a new limerick, his voice the very echo of David Attenborough.

'There once was a fellow called Peter
Whose neighbour was such a brow-beater
When she knocked on his door
He knew he was done for
And now Peter's a cold-omelette-eater.'

He lifts the ringing handset and sees from the caller ID that it is his father.

'Dad?'

'Just calling with an update, Peter.'

'How's mum? I was just about to call you.'

'She's had the hip replaced this afternoon and all's gone well. I'm hoping she'll be home by the weekend, they like to kick 'em out of hospital sharpish these days, don't they. She's still woozy from the anaesthetic, you know. She was asking after you when she came round.'

'I'll come up on the weekend.'

'That's three days away, son.'

'I'm sorry dad, I've got parents' evenings and work and house group – I just don't think I can get away until Saturday. Tell you what, I'll come on Friday night, straight from work.'

'Your mother wants to see you, Peter.'

'I'll be there. Sorry, dad – the door's just gone – I've got to go. Bye!'

Peter puts the receiver down and turns back to the telly. He opens his mouth and, magically, Bugs Bunny hops out, a rhyme at the ready:

'A young boy named Pete dreamed of spaceships
And of landing a plane on an airstrip
But his father made sure
That he took the grand tour
On a luxury tailor-made guilt trip.'

He settles back onto the sofa and finishes off his cold, blackened omelette while staring at a documentary about killer whales surrounding seals and rocking their iceberg platforms until they fall off and then eating them. He remembers reading once that killer whales aren't whales at all, but are actually dolphins, only people don't like the sound of killer dolphins, so they call them whales instead.

He is pulled back from his trance with the ping of a new text message arriving on his phone.

In the voice of a race commentator, Peter begins to speak to the empty room.

'And they're coming in now. Who will be first past the post for our quickest house group texter to reply? Instinct tells me to expect to see Mary's name in lights and I'm checking now and – yes – yes! It's Mary – Mary's answer has come in, she's miles ahead of the rest and, as ever, replying in the affirmative with the usual *I'll be there, Pete!*'

Peter changes accents to play the role of co-commentator now.

'Of course, Peter, experience has taught us to expect Mary's reply first but also to expect a second text on the actual evening of house group to announce her state of tiredness or ill health and consequent non-attendance.'

'You're right there, mate,' the first voice replies, 'Mary's attendance comes in level pegging with Tara's regular text – which, may I say, I'm expecting to see at any moment.'

Right on cue, Peter's phone pings: Tara's text has arrived.

Peter flicks his thumb across the phone screen and checks the second text: *I won't be able to make it this week – such bad luck! Tara xxx*

At least she is consistent, thinks Peter, and at least she replies.

As he climbs wearily into bed at midnight, Peter mumbles with the soft growl of Clint Eastwood:

'There once was a sad house group leader
Who texted round his usual pleader
But with just two replies
He was forced to surmise
That his group thought he was a mind reader.'

The next evening, Peter sees Jean on his doorstep as he pulls his car into the drive.

'I'm sorry, Jean, I'm only just back from work,' he says, 'I haven't had a chance to look at your paperwork yet.'

'It's not that, Peter.' Jean sways like washing in the breeze. 'It's the prayer meeting. It's tonight. I thought I'd hop in the car with you to save global warming.'

'But you don't have a car to cause global warming in the first place.' Peter stares at Jean, confused.

'Exactly. I'm already saving the environment. Now I'm going to help you to save the environment by saving petrol.'

'I was planning on saving the environment by not going,' Peter says, which makes Jean laugh.

'Oh, Peter, you always lift my spirits, you really do. I'll see you at seven,' she says, and goes back into her own home, like a cuckoo into a clock.

Peter reflects once more upon the mixed blessing of having a neighbour from church, then sighs and opens his front door.

'Well,' he announces to his empty house in the cheery tones of Terry Wogan, 'Shall we check the phone for replies? Let's do that.'

He pulls his mobile phone from his pocket and, in his best BBC newsreader voice announces, 'This just in, there are no replies – I repeat – no replies, that's zero in the way of replies, from Peter's house group. In the light of this completely shocking news we asked Peter how he was feeling about house group these days.'

'Well, Peter,' Peter replies to himself in a nasal tone, 'Increasingly I have to say my internal desire, that is, my deepest heart's wish, is to jack the whole flaming thing in.'

Peter is cut off by the ping of the phone in his hand. A familiar resentment rises within him when he sees Colin's name as the sender of this latest text.

I'm not sure if I can make it to house group tonight or not –

'Not sure, my eye,' he says out loud in his John Wayne drawl.

Would it spoil things if I don't come? Colin's text continued.

John Wayne's voice fills the hallway again, as Peter lets rip.

'No, Colin, it won't spoil things if ya don't come over tonight. In fact I won't miss ya if ya never come again, because ya only come twice a year anyway so why don'tcha just leave the group, ya no good lowdown dirty hustler?'

And then Peter types his reply into his phone: 'Not to worry. See you soon. Peter,' and he presses 'send' and it's done.

That night, Peter spits frothy bubbles as he brushes his teeth, the voice of Bruce Forsythe finding its way through the foam.

'A house group leader threw a fit
Said "I've had quite enough, I shall quit!"
When his group were surprised
He just rolled back his eyes
And replied simply, "You asked for it!" '

The phone wakes Peter at dawn on the day of house group. His heart races as he grabs the receiver by his bed in emergency mode, smearing drool across his face with his hand, expecting the worst, but it is his father calling to say his mother has improved and should be coming home for the weekend as planned.

At work, Peter receives three more texts from Mary. The first says, Looking forward to house group tonight! The second says, Work is really full on today! and the third says, Sorry Pete, it's all gone belly up here, I won't make it tonight as I'll be too exhausted.

In his lunch hour, Peter sits in a quiet corner of the staff room and looks through the Bible study for tonight's house group. He decides not to put too much time into it, as so far nobody has actually said they are coming.

Back home that evening, he boils the kettle and sets a few mugs out on the side, just in case. It is seven twenty-five. House group is due to start in five minutes' time.

At seven fifty, the doorbell goes. Amy, Joe, Steve and Lesley all arrive together. They are bright and bubbly and Peter loathes the sight of them with his whole heart at this moment.

They sit in his lounge and chat and laugh while, down the hallway in the kitchen, Peter makes drinks and finds a packet of biscuits.

As he enters the lounge, the old metal tray wobbling a little in his tight grip, no one looks up. He places their cups down before them.

'Steve - decaf tea; Amy, decaf coffee, two sugars; Joe, Earl Grey and Lesley, peppermint tea,' he says.

The group carry on talking. Amy picks up her drink without thanking its maker or supplier.

'This must be how God feels all the time,' Peter mutters under his breath, and returns to the kitchen to get some biscuits.

As he unwraps the Rich Teas (the group are long past deserving Hobnobs), Peter listens to his house group laughing in the lounge. He thinks about the six who aren't here tonight, four of whom he's heard nothing from.

He thinks about work and how he could really do with spending some time going over some reports this evening and how he might do that after the group have gone, and his heart sinks even lower as he thinks about how tired he will be by then, and how late it will be.

He thinks about Jean, who stood swaying on his step again earlier this evening, asking if he'd made any progress with the mortgage shortfall paperwork. What a mixed blessing it is, having a neighbour from church!

He thinks about his parents, and knows he needs to make the long drive to visit them this weekend, and wonders if he should be there to help his father get his mother safely home from the hospital, and whether he ought to speak to the head at school early in the morning, and see if he could possibly have the afternoon off.

Peter begins to feel angry. He slaps the biscuits on the plate, hard, breaking quite a few. He yanks the plate up from the worktop and storms back into the lounge, Rich Teas falling to the floor as his legs gather speed and momentum down the hallway. His house group are still laughing as they await their next delivery.

'Ah, biscuits - at last!' Joe says. 'We were beginning to give up on you, Pete!'

Something inside Peter snaps. He picks up a handful of biscuits and throws them at Joe. Then he throws some at Amy and Lesley, and, with just one biscuit left on the plate, he crushes it in his trembling fist over Steve's head.

His group stare up at him, mouths open, eyes wide, coated in broken biscuit crumbs, waiting for the punch line.

'Get out!' Peter screams at them, surprised at how mad his own voice sounds. 'GET OUT NOW!'

The four of them are up and stumbling towards the door, tripping over each other in their fight for coats and shoes as Peter stands there, shaking with rage and fear at what he is doing.

'Hey, we just –' Joe begins.

'OUT!'

As they scuttle down the path, shocked, silent, frightened, self-righteous and longing to tell everyone they have ever known about the last two minutes of their lives, Peter moves to slam his front door. A foot jams itself in the last wink of an opening.

'Pete?'

It is Steve.

'What?' Peter doesn't open the door at all.

'I just wanted to ask –'

'What? What? What could you possibly want to ask me?'

'I texted you on Wednesday to ask if you wanted to come out for a drink with me and the lads on Saturday. You didn't reply. Shall I take that as a yes?'

LET'S TALK

1. Do you think Peter would have gone for that drink on Saturday night? What would you like him to do after this story? How would you like the rest of his group to behave in the aftermath of his explosion?

    _____

    _____

    _____

    _____

    _____

2. If you could step into this story, knowing how Peter felt, what would you say to Jean, to Peter's father and to his house group? What would you say to Peter?

    _____

    _____

    _____

    _____

    _____

3. What does this story say to you about anger and losing your temper?

    _____

    _____

    _____

    _____

    _____

4. Have you ever been a small group leader, or any other kind of group leader, either at church or at work? How is the experience of running a group different from the experience of being a member of a group?

_____

_____

_____

_____

_____

5. In what ways do / could you support your house group leader? What about other leaders in your church?

_____

_____

_____

_____

_____

LET'S LISTEN

'Here is a simple, rule of thumb guide for behaviour. Ask yourself what you want people to do for you, then grab the initiative and do it for them. Add up God's Law and Prophets and this is what you get.'

Matthew 7:12

'My grace is enough; it's all you need. My strength comes into its own in your weakness.'

2 Corinthians 12:9

'Moderation is better than muscle, self-control better than political power.'

Proverbs 16:32

'When you're given a box of candy, don't gulp it all down; eat too much chocolate and you'll make yourself sick; And when you find a friend, don't outwear your welcome; show up at all hours and he'll soon get fed up.'

Proverbs 25: 16-17

'A person without self-control is like a house with its doors and windows knocked out.'

Proverbs 25:28

'Fear God, dear child – respect your leaders; don't be defiant or mutinous.'

Proverbs 24:21

'Leadership gains authority and respect when the voiceless poor are treated fairly.'

Proverbs 29:14

LET'S PRAY

Firstly, if you've read this story to explore as a group, I salute you for your bravery! This is scary territory - and any discussion needs to be handled thoughtfully, sensitively, tactfully and prayerfully.

❖ All the stories in this collection are about realistic people - flawed individuals; there is no black and white, right and wrong, or straightforward solution. We're all a mixture of baggage, experience, circumstance and more. Most times when problems occur between people, no malice is intended: we are simply human beings who get things wrong.

❖ In my own experiences of leadership, whether in church or work roles, I've found that the entire process requires bucket loads of grace, because people will let you down again and again - and I've grown increasingly conscious of the ways I've let leaders down myself, many times. I'm grateful for the grace I've received from those who've led groups I've been a member of. I'm also aware of how often those who lead house groups tend to be people with very busy lives generally, and how difficult and frustrating it can be to lead a group when members don't take time to communicate well.

❖ This may be a time to make peace with any one in your church or group who you have consciously fallen out with, lost your temper at or been rude to or impatient with.

❖ It may also be a time to acknowledge your need to forgive others for those times they've let you down, or to ask for forgiveness for letting people down yourself.

❖ As a group, pray together about any issues raised by this story. Put into action any thoughts on how to improve communications with each other, as well as ways to better support group leaders and facilitators.

❖ Finally, focus on the funny side: embrace the humour of this story, and be willing to laugh at how stressed out we can get, and how we can do ridiculous things in the heat of a lost temper!

PRAYER JOURNAL SPACE

REFLECTIONS, LEARNING POINTS AND IDEAS FROM THIS SESSION...

A FAMILY CRISIS

Edith Pinn has a secret fear, which is all under control
– until Tony Partridge joins her home group.

The day Tony Partridge joined our home group was the day everything went wrong for me.

I used to love home group, they were six of the nicest people I knew. We used to say we were small but perfectly formed. There was Violet and Terry, both in their seventies, both Street Pastors, an inspirational pair who'd fostered dozens of kids over the years. There was Bill and Barbara, both larger than life and great at organising social events to ensure we all stayed chummy. Then there was Norman and May: he'd been a vicar up North before they'd retired back down here where their kids all live. May bakes like a dream, and each week she delighted us with shortbreads, flapjacks, coffee cakes and tea-breads.

And then there was me: Edith Pinn. Just Edith, no middle name. Small, quiet, tidy. I seem to be one of those invisible people that no one ever remembers having met on a coach holiday or at a prayer meeting. I am Edith Alone; there's no other half: never has been, probably never will be. I don't mind that. Marriage never really appealed to me, which is fortunate because I've never appealed to anyone else enough for them to want to be married to me anyway.

As I say, things were perfect. We all got along, we all felt safe and comfortable with one another. I looked forward to every Thursday. I'd been leading the group for six years, and I had no plans of stopping any time soon. Things couldn't have been better.

But of course, the church leadership knew we were a very small group, and we all knew that the church was growing. Unfortunately this meant our idyll was about to be shattered.

When it was first suggested to me that we might take Tony Partridge on as our eighth group member, I hesitated. I didn't know anything about Tony. I wasn't sure he'd fit in. But Tony was keen. He came to try us out – *try us out!* That's what he said – as if he were test driving a second-hand car!

Well, he *tried us out* a few weeks ago, and everybody took to him right away, I must admit. Well, they're a friendly bunch. He said all the right things about May's flapjack, and he already knew Violet and Terry, because he's a Prayer Pastor with the Street Pastors, so he was well in there with them. And it turned out he'd gone to the same school as both Bill and Barbara, so he was well and truly one of the gang.

I couldn't put my finger on it at first, but there was something about him that didn't quite click with me. Of course it all made sense very soon, but at that point I just sensed something, and I held back from forming any opinions on Tony Partridge.

On his second visit, he picked up with people as if he'd been there for years. I felt he was overly friendly, to be honest. You know the sort, like an old fashioned shopkeeper, full of banter and cheek. Turned out he'd already been for supper to Bill and Barbara's, and May had baked flapjacks just for him this week, on top of the shortbread she'd made for the rest of the group.

Well, I told you they were a nice bunch of people. If they have any fault, it's that on occasion they're too nice.

It was while we were sipping our cups of Fair-Trade decaf coffee that Thursday evening that Tony dropped his bombshell and it all fell into place: he started talking about his pigeons.

Well, like I said, they're a friendly bunch; they asked him to tell them all about the birds. But I knew what was coming, and I suddenly understood the dread that had been balling in my stomach from the moment Tony Partridge had stepped into my lounge.

The room and all its faces sort of blurred and merged and then faded from my vision, and my eyes saw quite a different sight: a concrete yard; a cage; a shut back door; my hands over my eyes; terror: inside, I'm six years old again, back at the Baxters' house.

Mother and Father were great friends with the Baxters. The Baxters didn't have small children, their son was all grown up and moved away, so when we went there I was left to my own devices. They came to our church, that's how my parents knew them. Mr. Baxter played the organ, and his wife was in charge of the flowers.

They lived in a tidy two-bedroomed Victorian semi, and in their small, concrete-covered backyard there was a huge wire cage, filled with budgerigars.

One time when we went to the Baxters, it was a stiflingly hot day. The grown-ups needed to have an important conversation all alone without little ears anywhere within range. I needed to stay out of the lounge.

Mr. Baxter took me to the back yard.

'Here – come and meet my darlings,' he said, with a leering grin.

He opened the wire door to the aviary just enough to push me through.

'There you go,' he said. 'Have fun.' He locked the cage door from the outside and went back inside the house.

'Mr. Bax-' I started, but I was too slow and too quiet and too invisible somehow for Mr. Baxter to hear. The back door shut with a click that told me it was too late, I'd been abandoned. I was alone with the birds.

I didn't like it in this wire box. I wanted to get out. I tried the cage door. I couldn't get it open. I rattled it hard. Still it was shut. The rattling set the birds off. They flew wildly around my head. I put my hands over my ears. What if they pecked my eyes? I started crying. I screamed out desperately, salty tears and thick mucus filling my open mouth. No one came. No one would come. The back door stayed shut.

The wings and claws kept catching my hair, so I curled myself down into a tight ball, as tiny as I could be, and I tried to hide on the concrete floor of the cage. I could feel the feathers and the beaks going over my body.

By the time my father came out, I was covered in feathers, droppings, snot and tears. My body was shaking uncontrollably, and I'd wet myself.

'What on earth have you done?' Mr. Baxter was cross.

I tried to cuddle into Father's leg, but he pushed me away. Mother wouldn't touch me, I was so dirty.

'Silly girl!' My father sounded angry. He grabbed the top of my arm and held my head so that I saw the puddle of wee I'd made. 'Look what you've done! What do you say?'

'I'm sorry,' I said to Mr. Baxter.

I cried all the way home. My parents wouldn't speak to me until the next evening, they were that ashamed of me.

That was sixty years ago.

Back in my lounge I find now that while they've all been chatting, my eyes have gone watery and my vision's out of focus. I'm looking around the chairs from May to Barbara, to Norman and Bill, to Terry and Violet, but I can't focus on any of their faces. All I see is teeth directed at Tony Partridge.

'You ought to come and see them,' he says, pulling his lips back to form a terrifying grin.

'How many have you got?'

No, May, no! Please don't!

'I've got ten pairs at the moment.'

'And they're all in your back garden?'

'Yes – I built a loft for them there.'

'Can they come and go as they please?'

'They can, but they tend to stick together.'

'Do you race them?'

'Oh yes, I compete regularly...'

And on and on it goes, and all I want to do is run from the room, screaming. But this is my lounge, in my house, so I've nowhere to escape to.

I am trapped.

I'm wondering whether to fake sickness – I feel I might very well be sick anyway, so it wouldn't be entirely false, when Tony Partridge says the words I knew would come.

'You must all come over. I could host a home group evening and show you my darlings.'

'Oh,' I say, freewheeling wildly, improvising in a state of terror, my pace racing so fast and powerfully I feel I might burst open. 'It's early days yet, Tony, you don't know if you're actually going to join us, do you?'

'Well, I've really enjoyed my two weeks' trial with you all – if you've got space for me, I'd love to join your group.'

'Of course we've got space,' Bill says.

'That's wonderful,' Barbara says.

'Hmm,' I say, and then I run out of words and my mouth hangs open, silent.

There is no way on earth that Tony Partridge is joining our home group. Not under my leadership.

*****

On Sunday I'm late for church. I don't really feel like going at all, to be honest, but I force myself. Because I'm late, the only seat available is in the front row pew. I slide in and feel a warm hand pat my knee. I look up and realise with dread that I am next to May. I worry that she will want to talk about Tony. As the next song is announced, she clasps my hand and puts her lips to my ear.

'Come with me,' she says. My stomach seems to flip within me.

Together we walk past all the rows of swaying, singing bodies enjoying '10,000 Reasons,' and we don't stop until we're in the coffee area at the back, through the double doors. It smells of broken biscuits and the faded blue carpet's a bit sticky underfoot.

'Edith, what's wrong?'

'There's nothing wrong, May,' I say.

'I know you, Edith Pinn,' she says, 'and I know when something's up. What happened to upset you in home group the other night?'

'Nothing.'

'No, no, something happened.'

She's looking right into my eyes and I can't bear it. I turn away and look out of the window at the privet hedge that surrounds the church and the cars racing down the main road beyond. I wonder where everybody else goes on Sundays... shopping, I suppose. What else is there to do if you don't go to church?

'Come on, Edith. Whatever it is, this is your chance to share your burden. We'll support you in every way we can.'

I turn back and stare at her. Does she know already? I'm afraid she's found out somehow about the birds, about that day, about the dirt and the wetting myself and the mess I was in.

'What is it, Edith? Please, tell me.'

Can I trust May? Can I tell her about this awful, shameful part of me? I stare back at the cars passing by, and I think, if I tell May about my failure, she'll know that I don't trust God enough. After all, if I trusted him, I wouldn't worry about birds every second I'm out of the house, would I? I wouldn't be afraid at all, would I?

I study May's features: the laughter lines around the eyes; the coral painted lips; the curly grey hair; the pastel pink fleece... she looks like she's never had a day's trouble in her life. Could she understand the strength of my fear?

'You can trust me, Edith. As a vicar's wife, believe me, there's not much I haven't heard. I pride myself on being pretty much unshockable.'

She takes hold of my shoulders and stares intently at my eyes. '*Trust me, Edith!*'

I stare back at her for some moments more, and then I look at the floor.

'I am afraid of birds,' I say, and I realise I must've said it too quietly because she lowers her face to mine.

'You what? I'm sorry, Edith, I didn't hear you. What did you say?'

'I'm rather afraid of birds, May,' I say, louder, looking at her face, searching her reactions.

'Birds?' She frowns.

'Yes.'

'What, *all* birds? Or just big ones?'

'All birds. Anything with wings and claws and noise.'

'Oh, Edith – so you don't want to go to Tony's house and see the pigeons? Is that it?'

'It scares me, May.'

'Oh, Edith, you silly girl, come here.' She pulls me into her sagging bosom, but suddenly I want to run. She doesn't understand. She thinks I'm silly, just like Father did. 'Don't you worry about a little thing like that,' she says, 'I'm just the same about spiders. It's no big deal – there's no need to make more of it than it is. You'll be fine. Tony's great fun, you know. You'll probably have a lovely time and realise that there's nothing at all to be scared of. He's single, too, Edith. Quite a catch, I'd say! Cast your burdens upon the Lord, Edith, and forget all about it. Now, come on, let's get back in there before the sermon starts.'

She takes my hand and pulls me back into the church. I don't want to go. I don't want to go. I don't want to go. She pulls me along behind her.

Does she think I haven't prayed about the terror every day for the last sixty years?

Someone's on the platform at the front, and they're talking. We shuffle back into our seats. May makes me go in first, so I'm sandwiched between her and Norman, totally trapped. I try to blank out the scarlet noise filling my head and focus instead on the young man on the platform. He's rather scruffy, with a checked shirt that he hasn't tucked into his jeans, and he keeps waving his arms as he speaks. The arm waving means his shirt lifts up revealing a pale, hairy tummy that overhangs the waistband of his jeans. I focus on the fold of flesh and try not to feel May's presence to my left.

'...So, if you are someone who's carrying fear, who's living under the power of fear in any way, I want to appeal to you to come for prayer today, after the service. Jesus doesn't want you to live in fear. You must face your fears.' He looks around the room, and his gaze settles on me. No one ever looks at me: I'm invisible. Why did he look at me? 'Thanks,' he says. He gets down from the platform.

May grabs my arms and leans in.

'That's you!' she hisses. 'There you go – all sorted!'

'Thank you, May,' I say, and I get up.

'Where are you off to? Prayer's not until the end of the service.'

'Just nipping to the loo,' I say, suddenly realising what an awful busybody May is. I push past her stupid fat knees and head to the back of the church, being careful not to make eye contact with anyone else from my wretched home group on my way, through the double doors and out onto the main road. I walk fast, and I keep walking. The cars pass me, their radios blaring, drivers' arms hanging out of windows, cigarettes dangling from their fingers. I pass the park, the supermarket (which is heaving: so *that* is where everyone was going), I turn into the quieter residential streets and march on, quick as I can past the flowering almonds and cherry trees. I turn the final corner and with mounting relief hasten down my front path. I don't let myself burst into tears until I am inside my house, with the door safely shut behind me.

When I've stopped sobbing, I find my address book and ring the church office telephone number. I get the answerphone, of course, because they're all still in the service, and I wait until the beep stops.

'This is Edith Pinn calling. I just needed to let you know I won't be able to lead home group anymore, with immediate effect. Something's come up. A...family crisis. I'll be away for a while. I –'

And then the machine cuts me off. I twitch and fuss my way around the house, tidying slips of paper away, emptying the bathroom bin, bagging up slices of bread in pairs from the loaf I bought yesterday and filing them away in the freezer. When I pick up a pile of newspapers to sort through for recycling I have an idea.

I flip the pages of this week's edition over quickly until I find the local *What's On* listings. I run my finger down the column until I find what I'm looking for: ah, that's good – the Baptist Church is actually closer to my house than St. Mary's, and their service starts at eleven, which means I could enjoy a bit of a lie-in on a Sunday morning. That's much better: I've always found getting to church for ten o'clock a bit of a rush.

I thank God for giving me a way out and I fill the kettle with fresh water to boil. My heart rate finally seems to be slowing a little.

LET'S TALK

1. If you could talk to Edith, what would you say?

    _____

    _____

    _____

    _____

2. What do you think of May's response to Edith?

    _____

    _____

    _____

    _____

3. If you could talk to May, what would you say?

    _____

    _____

    _____

    _____

4. Edith's afraid that her fear will show others that she's not
    dependent upon God as she should be: what do you think of this?

    _____

    _____

    _____

    _____

5. In prayer we ask God for things - but then what next? If Edith did go for prayer, how might she experience God's healing in this area of her life?

_____

_____

_____

_____

6. Have you ever been released from fear in your own life, or seen it happen for somebody else?

_____

_____

_____

_____

7. Do you think we can pray for emotional healing in the same way we pray for physical healing?

_____

_____

_____

_____

LET'S LISTEN

'Give your entire attention to what God is doing right now, and don't get worked up about what may or may not happen tomorrow. God will help you deal with whatever hard things come up when the time comes...'

Matthew 6:34

'Steep yourself in God-reality, God-initiative, God-provisions. You'll find all your everyday human concerns will be met.'

Luke 12:31-32

'...I'm leaving you well and whole. That's my parting gift to you. Peace. I don't leave you the way you're used to being left – feeling abandoned, bereft. So don't be upset. Don't be distraught.'

John 14:27

'If you don't go all the way with me, through thick and thin, you don't deserve me. If your first concern is to look after yourself, you'll never find yourself. But if you forget about yourself and look to me, you'll find both yourself and me.'

Matthew 10:38-39

'God is love. When we take up permanent residence in a life of love, we live in God and God lives in us. This way, love has the run of the house, becomes at home and mature in us, so that we're free of worry on Judgment Day – our standing in the world is identical with Christ's. There is no room in love for fear. Well-formed love banishes fear. Since fear is crippling, a fearful life – fear of death, fear of judgment – is one not yet fully formed in love.'

1 John 4: 18

LET'S PRAY

Fear can be utterly crippling; it can make us feel ashamed, embarrassed, silly and guilty for our apparent lack of faith in dealing with it. It can tap into parts of our life from long ago which are deeply embedded in our secret histories, just as they were for Edith

❖ If fear has a hold on you in any way, and you'd like God to free you from its grip, begin that prayer process. However, be prepared that God will give you opportunities to step free from fear by trusting in him!

❖ Remember, he will never give you more than you can handle – which is to say, when your trust and dependence are fully upon him, you can handle anything!

❖ God is so kind and gentle towards us, tender as a loving father; he doesn't want to hurt you, he is on your side and longing to show you just how much he loves you.

❖ Start by talking honestly to God about the things you are afraid of. Feel free to write that prayer in the space provided here.

In your group discussion and prayer times for this story, don't feel you have to reveal everything that's on your heart; be wise in what you share, perhaps seeking a trusted friend to talk to one-to-one about anything particularly pertinent for you.

PRAYER JOURNAL SPACE

REFLECTIONS, LEARNING POINTS AND IDEAS FROM THIS SESSION...

DEGREES OF SEPARATION

When Bridget invites Tish for lunch,
she knows she's taking a huge risk:
will it be the disaster both women expect?

Please note this story contains an expletive; it has been used with consideration as it forms part of the content for discussion.

T ish

Sunday, 10:45am: Church.

I raise my head as I sense movement to my right. I turn and see the too-familiar sight of Jake and Seth being brought back to me by Amy, the Sunday school helper. For me, church is over.

I raise my eyebrows at Amy – what did they do this time? She smiles at me apologetically, shakes her head, shrugs her shoulders. I get up, take the twins' hands from her and lead them from the school hall where our church meets, out through the double doors towards the car park. I sigh, and turn back to watch Amy disappearing down the corridor, back to the kids' groups.

'What happened, boys?' I ask once we're safely outside the building, and out of earshot of any of the congregation.

'Nathaniel said Seth smells like farts,' Jake says.

'I don't smell like farts!' Seth is raging.

'Of course you don't. That was a horrid thing to say. What did the leaders do?'

'They didn't hear it.'

'They just saw me getting cross with Nathaniel.' Jake pouted at the injustice.

I sigh.

'What did you do?'

'He jumped on him like this –' Seth starts recreating the scene, holding Jake down on the grassy edge of the car park, and thumping his ribs.

'Ok, ok, that's enough of that,' I say.

'And then Jake said Nathaniel smells of shit,' Seth adds, glancing sideways at Jake who flies at him with both fists ready.

I stop dead in my tracks.

'You said what?'

As Seth starts to repeat Jake's phrase, I raise a hand, palm outward, like I'm stopping traffic.

'Enough! Where have you heard that word?'

'Dominic at school says it all the time,' Jake whines.

'I don't care what Dominic says,' I say, fighting to control my voice, 'You're seven years old and I do not want to hear you speaking that way again today or ever. Have you got that?'

Both boys start to protest, and I raise my hand again, finger pointing to the sky.

'Have. You. Got. That?'

They murmur assent and I sigh, long and heavy.

'Come on boys, let's go home.'

As I unlock our car I see Bridget sitting in her people carrier, breastfeeding that perfect little baby boy of hers, Toby I think he's called. It's a picture of contentment, and it pulls at the same old places within me, even seven years on.

Breastfeeding twins is...well, if you've ever done it, you'll know the word 'challenge' doesn't really come close. And if you've ever tried it in the midst of discovering your husband's having an affair with your best friend and everybody else knew about it except you, and you get mastitis repeatedly and let's not even get started on inverted nipples...It was bottles or a breakdown for me. A simple choice in retrospect, but the guilt of a failed breast-feeder is a secret pain with its own peculiarities.

Bridget's kids are all flipping perfect.

I turn to our tiny, clapped-out car: the boys are fighting over who gets to sit in the front, and I get over to them just in time to catch Seth's fist in the air, before it can make contact with Jake's cheek.

Bridget

Sunday, 11am: Church Car Park.

Oh, great.

I came out here to avoid the stares, and there's that woman with the crazy boys, gawping right at me. I bet she breastfed both those twins no problem.

I can't even manage one.

'But I'm gonna try my best, Toby, my love,' I say, kissing my little boy's peach-fuzz head.

Ellie and Mia both ended up on the bottle, despite my trying every possible tactic. This is my last chance to get it right – God knows I'm doing badly enough anyway with both the girls. Perhaps that bottled milk at birth was where it all went wrong? Perhaps they didn't bond with me enough, or get the right nutrients? I don't know. Everyone spouts reassurance, but I doubt their sincerity. People just say what they know I want to hear.

At five o'clock this morning I was in the lounge, working away with that awful breast pump, feeling like a cow in a dairy farm. An hour and a half of pumping, and I got a pathetic two ounces of milk. Toby's such a hungry boy, an ounce is barely a mouthful to him. At six forty five, I put the bottle on the side – stupidly, I admit – by the sink. I suppose I was tired and not thinking right. Tom got up to make a cup of tea and I watched him pick my hard-come-by milk up and tip it away down the plughole. He'd thought it was last night's formula dregs.

I suppose I can understand why he did it, but he didn't seem to appreciate just how soul destroying and heart-breaking that was for me. I burst into tears, he got defensive – and now we've got a huge row to sort out. We were still shouting at each other as we pulled into the church car park; the girls were upset; Toby was screaming in his car seat, crimson-cheeked and fists clenched in fury, and we all had to somehow walk into church as if nothing was wrong and everything was perfect.

What a mess.

Tish

Monday, 9:30am: Croft Primary School Pastoral Support Office.

I feel bad for Mrs Conway, stuck in this space that surely was once an actual broom cupboard.

The sign on the door says 'PASTORAL SUPPORT', but Rita Conway has been far more to me these last three years than a mere support. I've sat in this room and cried, and laughed, and despaired – and sometimes I've even dared to hope. Dared to hope that all the twins' behavioural issues are a phase that will, one day, be over. That they will enter a classroom without shouting or barging into anyone; that they will sit down without kicking chairs or tables; that they will get on with the work the teacher asks them to do without screwing up their paper and throwing it across the room, or scribbling on someone else's work...Well, I can dream.

Rita understands the twins so well, and she feels a lot of this behaviour is still payback from Darren walking out on us the week they started school.

I'm pretty sure me getting the TA job here last year is thanks to Rita.

She's late today, so I sit and check my diary. Just as I find the page for this week, she bursts into the room.

'I'm sorry, Tish,' she says. Her hair looks as if she's just fallen out of a tree.

'Everything OK?' My first thought is that this must be something to do with the twins. The permanent knot in my belly tightens in preparation for more bad news.

'Issues with a parent.' Rita exhales heavily.

I must confess, I'm relieved it's not my boys.

'Let me make you a tea,' I say, getting up and going to pump water into a *World's Best Teacher* mug from the vacuum flask that stands on top of the metal filing cabinet. I drop a teabag in and try to squeeze some colour from it, add some milk from the long life carton she keeps next to the flask, warming in the stale office air.

She sinks into her chair and shuts her eyes.

'I don't know how you do it,' I say.

'I don't know how *to* do it, a lot of the time,' she responds, eyes still closed.

I place the cup of pale dishwater-like liquid before her.

'Tea's here,' I say. 'If this is not a good time I can come back.'

She opens her eyes, rubs her forehead as if wiping away the memory of whatever just happened.

'Thank you, this is great.' She raises her mug in a small gesture of 'cheers', and smiles. 'Now, let's talk about your lovely boys. They've had a better week you know. It'll cheer me up to think about it.' She takes a deep slurp of the disgusting brew before her. 'Mmm, lovely. Always tastes better when someone else makes it for you, doesn't it?'

She smiles and shuffles through a pile of folders on her desk.

'Ah, here's Jake...' She shuffles deeper, '...And here's Seth. Excellent. First things first: how've things been at home this week?'

I feel the knot in my belly loosen somewhat as I begin to talk and reflect on the challenges of the last week.

Bridget

Thursday, 10a.m: Church Toddler Group

Why I keep coming to this group I do not know. I cannot wait until Toby starts school and I'm released from this imprisonment. I've done nine years' worth of Thursday mornings here.

Nine years! You'd think I might have made one friend in all that time, wouldn't you? But no. I've made an awful lot of familiar strangers. It's a level of familiarity that causes me to feel awkward all over town – at bus stops (I'm usually driving past – but there's always some poor woman and child pair that I know at a bus stop, only I don't have enough seats to offer a lift to more than one person, or if I only have Toby in the car I don't have another car seat – but I feel *so* bad about not offering lifts to people I recognise!), in cafés (I get my coffee, turn around and recognise a woman and child sitting there, she sees me: do I sit with her? I never want to – I don't even know their names, nor they mine. But is it rude of me to ignore them? Or would it be intrusive to assume? I never know. I never sit with them. I take my coffee as far as I can from them and sit feeling dreadful, fairly sure I've done the wrong thing, every time). I see them in the playground at school pick up (Do I talk to them? They all seem to be in gangs, while I'm the solitary one. They have kids Ellie and Mia's ages, but their kids never hit it off with mine, or I presume I'd know about it. Besides, I'm the one on my own. Couldn't someone else, just once, make the effort and come and talk to me?)

As my eyes wander around the room – children pottering, some happily, some angrily, with play-dough and building blocks and paint and sand - there are mothers breastfeeding, oh so casually, as if it were the easiest thing in the world. I try not to think hateful thoughts, I pray a quick prayer of apology for my envy and resentment.

Tish and her boys suddenly spring to my mind. I feel bad for Tish; her boys are a right handful, and she seems to be permanently on the fringes of church. Perhaps I should ask her for lunch...

I'll see her at school pick up - I'll see if I can catch her then. If God wants me to ask Tish for lunch, he'll make sure we bump into each other.

Tish

Friday, 3:15pm: School Playground

Bridget from church came striding up to where I was standing at the door today, releasing the children from my class back to their parents, and she said, 'Would you like to come to my house for lunch this Sunday?'

Well, I didn't see that coming! I couldn't think of any way of getting out of it, so I said yes.

So, my boys and I are off to Madam Perfect's house for lunch this Sunday. I'm feeling sick at the thought of it. I dread to think what the boys will do. It's going to be embarrassing.

I know already just how her house will be: tidy and tasteful and perfect. It's going to make me feel like crap and the boys will break something or spill something... and then I'll never be able to face her at church again.

Maybe we shouldn't go...?

Bridget

Friday, 6pm: Home.

I place the salad bowl on the table.

'Urrr!' comes the predictable cry of disgust. It's the last straw as far as I'm concerned.

'Right! Just take a slice of bread and eat it in front of the telly! I don't want to sit at the table and hear you complain about the food I've stood here for half an hour preparing for you!'

Ellie pushes her chair back with an ear-splitting scrape.

'Fine,' she growls, and she's gone.

'Great – what a great example,' Mike says.

'Well, maybe if you supported me a bit more and stood up for me I might feel a bit less stressed out at mealtimes.'

'Oh, don't turn this on me. What happened there was nothing to do with me at all.'

'If you're going to talk to me like that you can take your food to the lounge with Ellie,' I say, and I can already feel my eyes stinging.

'But I laid the table,' he says.

'Oh, you men! You do one job and you expect a medal for it!'

'Fine,' he takes his plate, splats the pasta bake onto it with a thwack that sends tomato sauce and melted cheese flying in every direction.

Mia grabs a plate and does the same.

'Hold on, Dad, I'm coming with you!' And she runs off, down to the telly.

I sit at the table for a few minutes, the tears threatening. How did that go so wrong so quickly?

It suddenly hits me: there's no way we can have Tish and her kids here for lunch: we can't have anyone for lunch – not with the rows and mood swings in this house! And at that thought, the tears come.

Then Mike comes back. He puts his hand on my shoulder.

'I'm sorry, love,' he says. 'I lost my rag.'

'No, it was my fault,' I say, 'I lose mine too easily.'

'Kids seem to know exactly which buttons to press.'

'But I let them press them too often. I know my weak spots and yet still I give in again and again. I pray about it, Mike, I really do - but it never seems to change.'

Mike calls the girls back to the table.

'Let's start again,' he says.

Ellie mumbles a rather mean sounding apology. It's the best I'll get, and I accept it. To change the subject, I mention the possibility of having guests for lunch on Sunday.

'Ooh!' Ellie brightens, to the relief of us all. 'Jake got sent to the headmaster today.' She's delighted with her news. Mike frowns.

'What for?'

'He swore at a teacher! And Seth made Sarah in my class cry yesterday,' she adds.

'I'm scared!' says Mia, hiding under the table.

'What are you scared of?' I say, wondering if Mia is afraid for the same reasons I am.

'They'll swear at me! They're always hitting people.'

'Well if they hit either of you two they'll have me to answer to,' Mike says, every inch the Alpha Male.

'I'm sure they won't hit either of you. Come on, we need to be nice to these people. We're going to be in heaven with them for eternity,' I say.

'I don't want to go to heaven with Jake and Seth!' Mia screams from under the table. 'They'll smash my face in for eternity!'

I look at Mike; he looks at me. Ellie watches us both. Thank God, Toby starts crying and I'm released to go and make a bottle up. For once, I'm grateful for the distraction of mixing formula.

Tish

Sunday, 12 noon: Church Car Park.

Today's was a family service – which was a relief. At least I knew the boys wouldn't be sent out of Sunday school in disgrace. Mind you, they fidgeted their way through the sermon and, even with me sat between the two of them, they still managed to wind each other up. My thigh muscles are killing me from straining to keep them as far apart as possible. It didn't help that the man in front of us was clearly suffering with wind this morning, of the silent-but-deadly variety. The boys made a huge show of wafting their hands beneath their noses, pinching their nostrils and faking death. In the end their giggles were so obvious I took them out myself.

On my way out I saw Bridget – breastfeeding again out in her car. She spends her life breastfeeding, that Bridget. Her boy should certainly be well bonded to her: he's permanently on the boob.

She mouthed, 'See you soon,' through the car window at me, and I smiled and gave a thumbs-up and lied, 'Yeah, great – looking forward to it.' I know I'm going to come away from hers feeling awful about myself and my life and my sons and everything else.

I wish I wasn't someone who thought this way. I'm well aware that Bridget and I will be spending eternity together, and so it would be a good idea to get past the formalities ahead of time. It's just so hard to love people in church, somehow. It's hard even just getting to *know* them, frankly. Pretty much everyone in church knows nothing about me. And, I suppose that must mean I don't know much about them, either.

But Bridget and I – we're worlds apart.

Bridget

Sunday, that patch of time between church and lunch: the kitchen.

Why, oh why, oh why did I choose to do a roast? What was I thinking? Everyone knows a roast is all about timing and that timing is impossible when you've spent three hours in church! Why didn't I just do sausages? Or pizzas? That way the kids would probably eat them, too!

At the very least I should have bought readymade Yorkshire puddings!

And Mike is bog-all help with either the kids or the cooking. He tried to get involved a minute ago, but he seems unable to understand the concept of reading a recipe book and following it for himself. He spent three minutes picking up and putting down a pan, a pint of milk, a packet of bread sauce mix and a whisk, staring at each and asking me repeatedly, 'What do I do now?' In the end I pulled the packet mix from his hand and sent him off to clear some of the junk from the dining table so it can at least be laid.

The girls are bickering in the front room over some terrible problem with a make believe world they're playing with on the tablet. Why doesn't Mike go and deal with that instead? Why am I the one who has to say 'no' all the time?

And why aren't my roast potatoes browning? They're just staying pale. What's that about? They still look raw, but they need to come out in five minutes for the Yorkshires to go in!

Why did I do a roast?

Oh Lord, gravy! Gravy! I'm terrible at gravy! I forget how to make gravy every time I need to make it! Why can't there just be one way to make gravy that we stick to all the time, like toast or cereal; just a formula. Do they make packet mix gravy? I bet they do, these days. Why didn't I think of that?

I hope those boys are going to be ok, I really do. They're just unknown quantities to me, boys. Girls, I get. Emotional torment, psychological agony, hormonal hell – I'm used to all that. Boys... well, I suppose I'll learn as Toby grows up. But twin boys? That's something else. At least at seven they'll be potty trained. Goodness knows, I couldn't take any poo dramas this afternoon. I've had enough of those to last a lifetime.

And just as I'm thinking about all the poo dramas I've survived, Mia walks into the kitchen and stands behind me, and I can smell it coming off her.

'Do you need a poo, Mia?'

'No.' The firm face of denial that always signifies the opposite is true.

'You smell like you need a poo.'

'Don't.'

'Listen, you're not going to do your usual, are you? You're five years old, Mia, you should be well past all this by now! I don't want to find that you're pooping in your pants while we've got guests here, and I won't be able to take you to the loo and spend hours cleaning you up once they've arrived. So if you need a poo, I suggest you go and have one now.'

'Don't need one!' She shouts and pouts and stomps away.

And then the doorbell goes.

Tish

Lunchtime: Bridget's House.

I knew they'd have a nice kitchen. I just knew it. Wooden tops and butler sink and wood flooring and all the stuff. Big Miele dishwasher. Fancy five-ringed stove. A burglar could be forgiven for assuming Mary Berry lived here.

I admit it, I'm feeling envious. I'm already praying silently for forgiveness and asking God to make me content with what I have on my way through to the kitchen when I pass the lounge: it is a deep red, with pictures and a plush, bright blue sofa. A brave choice of colours, but it really works. I think about our magnolia lounge with its thin rug over the cheap laminate. Maybe I should repaint... thing is, when you start with a beautiful Georgian semi, you can't go far wrong. With mine, you're starting with a 1960s ex-council box, lacking in style or character. You're onto a loser from the off, really. Best to keep the magnolia; anything else will just draw attention to what's lacking.

And, of course, the food is perfect. A perfectly roasted chicken, glistening and golden; Yorkshire puddings all risen evenly and just the right side of crispy. Ok, so the potatoes could have done with ten minutes more, but they still look pretty darn good. The crockery is beautiful and the glasses are crystal.

Her kids are polite, shy... quiet. She has no idea how lucky she is!

Mind you, Jake and Seth are being fairly subdued, too. They seem particularly shy of Mike.

Actually, Mike isn't doing much, I can't help but notice. It's not like he's helpful to Bridget, who's fussing over some gravy at the stove, and he's not even picking up baby Toby, who's clearly tired and needing to be taken upstairs. I get the feeling Bridget's waiting for Mike to take the baby. But Mike's drinking coffee and checking his phone. Adrian used to do that all the time, he drove me mad with it. I'm reminded of what he was up to on his phone all that time, and feel the need for a distraction.

'Can I stir that?' I ask Bridget, and she seems relieved to be able to leave the gravy in someone else's hands. She takes Toby upstairs to put him down for his nap.

All the time she's gone, Mike's on his phone.

Ellie and Mia still aren't talking to Jake and Seth, just staring at them. My boys are standing right behind me, pressing into a buttock each. I'd be embarrassed, but I know Mike's not paying any attention. He puts his coffee cup down without looking, and misses the worktop. The cup hits the floor and bounces - thankfully not breaking - but coffee splashes out all over the place.

'Damn!' he says, and then, to my utter amazement, he calls out, 'Bridget!'

Bridget comes down, sees the mess, sighs and gets a cloth from the sink and starts wiping it. I can't believe what's happening in here! Poor Bridget, she's basically a single parent with an annoying man hanging around her house getting in the way. Why does she take that? I'm sure I heard she was a solicitor or something before she had kids; why is she putting up with this?

And then, while she's cleaning, her eldest, Ellie, says 'Mum, I can see your builder's bum!' Her second girl, Mia, starts laughing, hard. Mike does nothing to defend her, but instead says 'Oo-er missus,' and starts giggling with the girls.

Jake and Seth grip tighter to my bottom. They're not used to this sort of talk in the home, joking at their mother's expense. I've always taught them this sort of thing is cruel. My cheeks are flaming on Bridget's behalf.

Maybe it's not so perfect here, after all. I pray a silent prayer for forgiveness for feeling smug and judgemental.

'Come on now, Ellie, stop that,' Bridget says, and I can hear from her voice that she'd like to shout at them. I'm sure she would if we weren't here, I know I would. In response, Ellie tuts and flounces out of the room, stepping over her mother cleaning the side of the swing bin. If this is what girls are like, thank God I had boys.

'Mummy,' Jake says quietly, pulling at my jumper.

'Yes, darling?'

'We don't say things like that, do we?'

I cringe.

'I'm sorry,' Bridget hauls herself to standing. 'She's a bit hormonal, I think. The teenage years seem to kick in around two years' old in girls.'

If she were mine, that child would be back in this room apologising. And Mike would be the one cleaning up the bin, instead of back on his phone as if nothing's happened.

My boys, on the other hand, are sweetness and light. It's as if they've had personality transplants. No kicking, no punching, no pinching, no throwing food, no bashing each other under the table when we finally sit down. Jake even tells a story about a teacher at school that makes everyone – including Mike – laugh.

Bridget

Dining Room, 2pm: Dessert

When did Mike become so completely socially inept?

I can hear myself babbling on in this stupid high pitched voice that doesn't sound like me at all and I'm talking so much that it's like I'm on overdrive having some sort of manic meltdown, and it's not until Ellie interrupts me with a 'Something's burning,' that I even remember the apple crumble in the oven.

I push my chair back too fast and it falls over.

'Oops! Easy, Tiger,' Mike says. I smile instead of delivering the slap I'd like to. Tish looks like she wouldn't mind slapping him either; I catch just a flicker of an eyebrow, but it's enough to let me know she disapproves. She's probably thanking God that she doesn't have a husband right now. Oh, God – forgive me for saying that. I don't know where these awful thoughts come from.

I put my chair right again, and open the oven door to get the crumble. A blast of smoke rushes out and sets off the smoke alarm above. I slap a tea towel at it until it stops, then turn my attention back to the crumble: its edges are crusted and black. I forgot to get custard, but I do find a tub of cream in the fridge. It's two days over its best before, so I pull the lid off and bin that, then give it a quick stir and sniff: it smells fine, absolutely fine. I'm sure it'll be alright. I hope so. I put it on the table.

I turn back to the crumble. Rescuing it would mean hacking off the entire crumble layer. It'll just have to go out as it is.

'Eww,' comes Ellie's predictably disgusted response. 'Burnt again. Mum burns everything.' She rolls her eyes as if I were a naughty child.

'Excuse me young lady,' I say, unsure of how to finish that sentence in front of guests.

'What? It's true, you do,' Ellie replies, full of challenge. I look at Mike: he's checking his phone *again*! I want to take that phone and drop it into the cream pot – except I can't because we need that cream. How could I be so stupid to forget the custard? Maybe I'll shove his phone deep into the crumble, till the sticky apple fills the plug-in charger hole bit...

I look at the crumble. I look around the table. It's very, very clear from the wide eyes and biting of lips that's going on that no one wants to eat my food under any circumstances.

'Kids – there's a Chocolate Orange in the cupboard – why don't you take that through to the lounge and you can play while you eat it.'

'Whatever,' Ellie says, running to the cupboard to get the Chocolate Orange before anyone else. Just as I'm feeling things can't get any worse, Mike gets up and leaves the table with the girls! But the final nail in my coffin, the thing that really makes me long for death, is when Jake and Seth get up and *clear their plates from the table*. They put them by the sink (no hope of fitting anything else in there, it's full of pots and pans), and then they turn and they say – they actually say – '*Thank you.*'

Tish

Bridget's Kitchen Table, 2:15pm: Coffee

Thank goodness the kids have got down, and Mike, too. I couldn't have managed much more of that. I don't know what's going on with Bridget, she's completely manic. And I thought I was wound up tight!

I'm sitting here with the coffee Bridget's just made me, staring at her untouched, very burnt crumble. She sighs and slumps into the chair opposite me, and she looks like all the air has gone from out of her, like she's deflating.

'Your boys are so polite,' she says, staring at her coffee.

'That was a rare moment,' I say and laugh, although that's not true – I realise suddenly that my boys are quite polite, generally - but I don't want Bridget to feel bad. This can't have been an easy lunch for her.

'Girls are so... emotionally complicated,' she says, and she picks up her spoon and begins digging at the crusty crumble. Shards of hard, burnt edge fly out as she chips away. I take my spoon and do the same. Together, we bash the crumble.

'I was always a complicated one,' I say. 'Still am.'

'Me too,' says Bridget, and she smiles naturally for the first time since we got here.

'I'll tell you what I want, what I really, really want,' I start to sing, I don't know why I do it, but Bridget's eyes light up.

'Spice Girls! I loved the Spice Girls.'

'Me too – I went to see them live three times.' I smile, proud now of what I'd felt embarrassed by for a few years in my mid-twenties.

'So did I – three times! Where did you see them?'

'Birmingham –'

'Did you go to the Spice World tour at the NEC?'

'Yes! What night did you go?'

'I went on the Saturday. My auntie took me.'

'Me too! My friend's mum took us – it was such an amazing night.'

'I couldn't believe it when Geri left so soon after,'

'Me neither, I felt like my world had collapsed!'

'Remember when they got us chanting Girl Power! Girl Power!?'

'I remember.' I take a slurp of coffee. 'I have to say, I think feminism's all gone a bit wrong these last twenty years, though.'

'Don't get me started! It's so hard raising girls now, you know? All their role models are these skinny, make-up-plastered plastic looking people who bang on and on about how looks don't matter, all the while switching boyfriends quicker than I change my socks and getting parts of their body surgically enhanced... It's a tough time to find your identity as a woman.'

'I know – I feel like a broken record with the way I go on to the boys about the importance of respecting women.'

'I worry so much about Ellie and Mia.' Bridget stares at her spoon. 'Sometimes I get so scared about all the things that could go wrong, I wish we'd never even had children.'

'I thought I was the only one who felt like that.' I smile at Bridget through watery eyes.

'Whatever happened to 'happy ever after' eh?' Bridget reaches out for my hand and gives it a squeeze.

'Whatever happened to my *Prince Charming?*' I squeeze back.

'Well, after today, you can have mine.' Bridget starts to giggle. That sets me off.

'Family, eh?'

'Family.'

I felt the tension of the mealtime evaporating, like steam rising from my tight shoulders, loosening everything up. 'We ought to do this more often. I've never been to anyone from church's house for dinner.'

'Never? Are you serious? How long have you been coming to church now?'

'About four years. I think it must be because the twins are a bit of a handful. And perhaps –' I hesitate, search Bridget's eyes and see compassion there. 'I think maybe people are a bit hesitant with me being a single parent, they like to have even numbers round the table. Someone for their husband to talk to, maybe?'

'Gosh, church is so weird, isn't it?' Bridget sighs and leans back in her chair.

'Have you ever read –'

But I never get to share my book recommendation with Bridget because, at that moment, the shouting begins in the other room.

The shouts grow louder as four children fight each other on their way from the lounge to the dining table. They explode into the room, all arms, legs and wide-open mouths. Upstairs, Toby has been woken prematurely and is complaining about that by screaming.

'Where's your father?' Bridget says to the room; no one takes any notice.

Ellie's trying to say something, but Mia keeps pulling her arms away and fighting to shove her own hands over her sister's mouth.

'Mum –'

'No!' Mia pushes Ellie away.

'But, Mum!' Ellie persists.

'No!' Mia shoves her as hard as she can.

That's the moment when Jake and Seth push their way between the girls, eyes wide, mouths wider, their faces a picture of shock.

'Mia's done a shit on the rug!' They shout in perfect unison.

LET'S TALK

1. '...We were still shouting at each other as we pulled into the church car park; the girls were upset; Toby was screaming in his car seat, all red-faced and fists clenched – and we all had to walk into church as if nothing was wrong and everything was perfect...'

   Why do you think Bridget felt they had to walk into church 'as if nothing was wrong and everything was perfect'? Do you feel this is the best approach in the circumstances? Do you feel a pressure to appear as if everything is 'perfect' when you go to church? How would you advise handling the situation Tish and her family found themselves in?

   _____

   _____

   _____

   _____

   _____

   _____

2. Tish views Bridget's life and family as perfect before she goes to lunch at her house and the illusion is shattered. Do you think it's a good thing that she stops seeing Bridget in a false light, or do you prefer not to know the details of another's reality? Why, or why not?

   _____

   _____

   _____

   _____

   _____

   _____

3. 'It's just so hard to love people in church, somehow. It's hard even just getting to *know* them, frankly...' What would you say to Tish if you could have a chat with her about how she feels?

    _____

    _____

    _____

    _____

4. Both Bridget and Tish worry a bit in this story about spending eternity together – how did you respond to this part of the story?

    _____

    _____

    _____

    _____

5. Have you ever been surprised by the things you've discovered you have in common with others in your church?

    _____

    _____

    _____

    _____

6. 'Mia's done a shit on the rug!' This expletive is a shocking end to the story. What do you think about 'bad' language generally? Do you feel attitudes towards it have changed over recent years?

    _____

    _____

    _____

    _____

7. What do you think happens to Bridget and Tish after the end of this story? Will the women retreat from each other, or will this be the start of a deep and honest friendship?

_____

_____

_____

_____

LET'S LISTEN

'This is my command: Love one another the way I loved you. This is the very best way to love. Put your life on the line for your friends...'

John 15:12

'Here is a simple, rule-of-thumb guide for behaviour: Ask yourself what you want people to do for you, then grab the initiative and do it for them. Add up God's Law and Prophets and this is what you get.'

Matthew 7:12

'Later Jesus and his disciples were at home having supper with a collection of disreputable guests. Unlikely as it seems, more than a few of them had become followers. The religion scholars and Pharisees saw him keeping this kind of company and lit into his disciples: "What kind of example is this, acting cozy with the riffraff?"

Jesus, overhearing, shot back, "Who needs a doctor: the healthy or the sick? I'm here inviting the sin-sick, not the spiritually-fit."'

Mark 2:15-17

LET'S PRAY

Pray for greater honesty and acceptance between members of your church, and greater courage in making ourselves vulnerable in ways that ensure honesty in our relationships within the church.

❖ Pray against judgemental attitudes and division between the Christians in your community.

❖ Pray for solidarity, understanding and love between Christians worldwide as we seek to live in love as Jesus commanded.

PRAYER JOURNAL SPACE

_____

_____

_____

_____

_____

_____

_____

_____

_____

_____

_____

_____

_____

_____

_____

_____

_____

_____

REFLECTIONS, LEARNING POINTS AND IDEAS FROM THIS SESSION...

GRAHAM STOOD BY THE COT

Graham is preaching on healing next Sunday,
but right now he's in hospital with his wife and baby daughter.

Graham stood by the cot, with its clear plastic sides, and swallowed down a sob. His eyes followed the lines of wires (*so many of them!*) from the machines that beeped and flashed and monitored and measured, all the way to his baby daughter's tiny body.

She was more surgical tape than flesh. Three days old and still un-held. From the moment she'd entered the world in a dramatic rush that had required eleven medical staff, an ambulance, an anaesthetist, a surgeon and a knife, her life had been hanging by a thread.

'Good morning, Mr. Tattershall,' the ward's Matron liked to keep things formal and Graham had realised by now that she was never going to call him by his first name. She consulted the machinery surrounding his daughter. 'She's doing fine. All stable. Have you seen your wife this morning?'

'I've just come down from her ward.'

'How's she doing?'

Graham wiped his eyes, took a deep breath.

'Still weak, but getting there.'

'That's good.'

She turned from the machines to face him. Her eyes were the palest blue, like ice against her dark lashes. He wondered if he would ever know the colour of his daughter's eyes. He cleared his throat.

'How long do special care babies normally stay here for?' Even as he asked he knew it was a stupid question. It would take as long as it took, and if he got to take both Rachel and Rosie home at any point soon after all they'd been through, it would be the best day of his life.

The Matron was patient.

'It differs from case to case, Mr. Tattershall. We'll do our very best for Rosie, but in terms of timing – well, that's out of our hands. Are your work understanding about your situation?'

'Oh, yes, I think so. People are being very kind.' Graham's stomach muscles tightened at the memory of having got very cross with his PA that morning: she'd been trying to help, but tiredness and utter helplessness had got the better of him and he'd exploded with her over a trifling matter. He would have to go back to the office and apologise.

'What do you do, Mr. Tattershall?'

'I'm a pastor.'

'Pastor? Of a church?'

'That's right. The King's Church in town. Do you know it?' He braced himself for the response he often got when people found out he was a pastor; his official job title was in fact 'Elder', but nobody ever understood that term, there was just no cultural reference for it that people could latch on to. More often than not, it seemed to lead to bizarre conversations about forest communities of elves and fairies.

Graham found that conversations very quickly switched from either chummy to chilly or from chilly to chummy when the company he was in discovered he was a pastor. The temperature of the reaction depended on the company's entire lifetime of baggage in terms of church experience. Every encounter with every Christian was brought up at such times – or else there was nothing – he wasn't sure which response he preferred. Sometimes there was a rather patronising 'How nice,' followed by a hasty retreat. How would the Matron react?

'I know it. I go to St. Mary's in Broomfield.'

'Oh yes, St. Mary's. Excellent chap there, I hear. Brian, isn't it?'

'Reverend Jefferson is a very good man. He does a lot of hospital visiting, actually – would you like me to direct him your way?'

'Oh, I don't know. I'm probably okay, I think.' Graham began adjusting the thin blanket over his daughter's tiny legs. They were more like chicken wings than human limbs, he thought.

'Well, let me know if you change your mind.'

She glanced once more at the monitors and padded away, her rubber shoes squeaking against the blue linoleum floor.

Graham kept vigil over Rosie's cot for the rest of the morning. At noon, he settled into a chair next to her and dozed off. He'd slept so little for the last few nights, he wasn't sure which day it was. He needed to speak to his P.A. soon, to apologise properly for this morning, but right now, his eyes refused to stay open...

'Hello?'

Graham woke with a start, feeling the weight of a hand on his shoulder.

'Whatsawhasz,' he mumbled, blinking and jerking his head around until the nurse in front of him came into focus.

'Graham? It's me, Nurse Peters.'

'Is everything alright?' Panic set in, Graham lurched forward.

'Matron just wanted you to know that we're going to take some tests now to establish Rosie's vital signs. These tests will give us a good picture of exactly where she's at, and they'll tell us whether she needs another blood transfusion.'

'Right. When? Right now?'

'In about half an hour, Graham.'

'Ok. I'll pop up and let my wife know.'

Graham brushed the creases from his shirt and wiped his eyes with his palms, looked over the plastic cot side at Rosie, kissed his finger and touched it to her knee – the only part of her that didn't have wires attached to it – and left the cubicle.

The walk to his wife's ward took him down endless straight corridors with blue rubber floors and walls covered in artworks that were randomly bland or downright peculiar with neither rhyme nor reason so far as Graham could tell. Nothing soothed his hot eyes.

After a half mile of corridor he stopped at the lift and pressed the 'call' button. The thought crossed his mind, what if the lift breaks down with me in it? Picturing himself stuck, unable to care for Rosie or support Rachel was too awful to contemplate. He headed back off down the corridor to the stairs.

Three flights up he joined another corridor, this one covered in yellow rubber rather than blue. His wife's ward was quiet, full of people whose energy was being drawn into every heartbeat, and each breath.

Rachel was staring at the ceiling when he came to her cubicle. She'd been crying again, her puffy, red-ringed eyes gave her away.

'They're going to do more tests now.' Graham perched on Rachel's bed, laid his hand on her thigh. She also had wires attached to each hand, and small pads on her chest where they'd been monitoring her. 'I thought we should pray,' he spoke softly, almost whispering.

Rachel nodded her assent, and reached for his hand. Graham prayed and Rachel wept and together they pleaded with God for their daughter's life and health, until Rachel's tears slowed and she fell into another drug-fuelled slumber. Graham slowly lifted his weight from the bed and snuck out of the cubicle to walk the long corridors back to Rosie's ward.

On his arrival at the baby unit, he was met with smiles from the Matron.

'Mr. Tattershall, the test results are amazing – it appears that Rosie's recovery is perhaps happening much quicker than expected.'

The relief was too great. Graham reached for the nearest chair – one of the nurse's swivel desk chairs – and collapsed into it.

'Praise God,' he said. 'Thank you, God.' Then, '"*Perhaps*"?'

The Matron squatted down and laid a hand on his arm, and her expression grew serious. 'I'd like to run the tests again, with your permission, to double check the results we received. They really are nothing short of miraculous, but of course there's always the small possibility that they might be wrong.'

'Wrong? But you've run them right, haven't you? And I've been upstairs with Rachel, we've been praying.'

'We'll run the tests again, just to confirm everything. It'll take about twenty minutes. Perhaps you'd like to wait in the lounge area and I'll come and find you.'

Graham wandered through to the lounge. His body felt full of tiredness, like he'd been stuffed with hot cotton wool. He pulled out his mobile phone and tapped into his diary. He had a sermon to prepare for Sunday. It hung over him like a distant cloud on the horizon. He wasn't sure whether today was Thursday or Friday.

He sensed somebody else entering the room, but didn't look up.

'Mind if I join you?' The man's voice cut through his thoughts.

'Of course not, please, sit down.' Graham shifted in his seat and gestured to the rest of the chairs. The man sat next to him.

'I understand you're Graham Tattershall, from King's Church?' The man spoke gently.

Graham looked up. 'I am.' He looked at the older man, who was vaguely familiar. 'Do you have a child on the ward?'

'No – I'm Brian Jefferson – from St Mary's Broomfield. I heard that your wife and daughter are both under care here at present and wondered if I might pray for you?'

'Brian – of course! I'm sorry – we did meet at that Churches Together event last year, didn't we? I'm so sorry, I'm not quite with it at the moment.'

'Of course not, don't worry, quite understandable. I'd be a wreck in your shoes.'

'Well, I've just had a bit of good news actually. They've run some tests on Rosie and her vital signs are all looking very good. It's a real answer to prayer.'

'Praise the Lord.'

'Absolutely, and Amen to that.'

'That's wonderful. So you're just taking a few minutes to relax. You must be exhausted?'

'I was just thinking about this Sunday. I'm down to preach.'

'Could anyone stand in for you?'

'Well, I think it might be an ordained appointment, actually. I'm beginning a new sermon series on healing, of all things. It seems that God is writing my sermon for me!' Graham chuckled at the way God worked, but Brian only smiled gently.

'Well, if you'd like any prayer, I'm very happy to sit and pray with you.'

'Thanks, but I think we're fine now.'

The Matron's rubber shoes squeaked into the room.

'Mr. Tattershall?'

Graham smiled up at her, using facial muscles that had not been exercised yet this week. 'Yes?'

The Matron sat down opposite him.

'Hello, Julia,' Brian Jefferson spoke warmly to his parishioner.

'Reverend.' she smiled efficiently, and turned back to Graham, rearranging her features as she did so. 'Mr. Tattershall, are you happy to speak about your daughter's health with the Reverend here?'

'Yes, yes, it's fine.' Graham continued smiling, trying to ignore the distant alarm bell that had started quietly ringing at the back of his mind.

'Mr. Tattershall, we've had the results of the second test.'

'Yes?'

'I'm afraid those first results were somehow compromised.'

'Compromised?' His eyes held contact with hers for what felt like minutes.

'The test results were incorrect. I'm sorry to say the second test has unfortunately confirmed what we'd suspected: Rosie will need a further blood transfusion, and we're looking at at least six more weeks of intensive care.'

'But the first tests –'

She lowered her eyelids and spoke to his shoes.

'It happens sometimes.' She raised her eyes to meet his, and Graham saw pain there, an empathy that surprised him. 'I'm so sorry.'

'But –'

'We'll continue doing our very best for Rosie.'

He looked at the Matron and the Reverend through watery eyes. 'I know God's actions are not about my performance, and that it's all about grace, I know that in my head, but right now, at this moment, I can't help but wonder...'

He left his sentence hanging in the air.

'In my experience, miracles take a while.' The Matron placed her hand in his. She smiled, sadly. Graham nodded.

'They never did in the Bible, did they, though? People just got up and walked, didn't they? Or rose from the dead like the alarm clock had just gone off and nothing had happened... I've got to preach on this on Sunday. I have absolutely no idea what I'm going to say.'

He let his hand slip from the Matron's, rose and walked from the lounge. He placed one foot in front of the other until he found himself in the hospital café, safely surrounded by the noise and clatter of life.

He got a coffee and perched on a high, uncomfortable stool at a small round, sticky table. He stared into the space around him for a few moments, until his eyes began gradually to focus on details.

A few feet in front of him, two tables had been pulled together. Three women sat there with three children in wheelchairs. One woman held her child's head back to stop it from hitting the table as the boy – perhaps eight years old – seemed to have no control over his body. The woman held a cup to his lips and dabbed the drink from his chin when it ran back out of his mouth.

The second woman held a large syringe which she was topping up with baby milk. The milk travelled down a tube directly into the stomach of a girl who was perhaps ten years old. The girl's hands were clenched tight in the air, waving wildly. Her tongue flicked in and out of her mouth. The woman feeding her took hold of the child's clenched hand to keep it from knocking the tube of milk, and gently stroked the girl's sore-looking fingers.

The third woman was cuddling a boy with ear defenders on, who swallowed tiny mouthfuls of juice through a baby cup. Thick-lensed glasses were secured to his head with a band.

The three women chatted lightly, smiling all the time. They kissed the heads of the children they were with and laughed with genuine delight when the children responded in any way.

Graham let his coffee go cold. He left the café to go and find Rachel, and tell her the news.

LET'S TALK

1. Share your thoughts and reactions to this story.

    _____

    _____

    _____

2. Did any of Graham's experience ring true for you?

    _____

    _____

    _____

3. Graham can't help but feel there might be some connection between his 'performance' and his prayers. What do you think about this?

    _____

    _____

    _____

    _____

4. '...In my experience, miracles take a while.' The Matron placed her hand in his. She smiled, sadly. Graham nodded.
    'They never did in the bible, did they, though? People just got up and walked, didn't they?...'
    How do you react to these thoughts expressed by the Matron and Graham?

    _____

    _____

    _____

5. Does a fear of lack of instant or guaranteed results ever hold you back from praying for healing?

_____

_____

_____

_____

6. Have you ever prayed for healing for yourself or others? What happened?

_____

_____

_____

_____

7. At the end of the story, Graham is challenged in a way that overwhelms him: how did the ending of the story make you feel?

_____

_____

_____

_____

8. Healing is such a sensitive, controversial and challenging area – is it something you are pursuing or avoiding? Why, or why not?

_____

_____

_____

_____

LET'S LISTEN

'You don't need more faith. There is no 'more' or 'less' faith. If you have a bare kernel of faith, say the size of a poppy seed, you could say to this sycamore tree, 'Go jump in the lake,' and it would do it.'

Luke 17:6

'In prayer there is a connection between what God does and what you do. You can't get forgiveness from God, for instance, without also forgiving others. If you refuse to do your part, you cut yourself off from God's part.'

Matthew 6: 14-15

'Don't bargain with God. Be direct. Ask for what you need. This isn't a cat-and-mouse, hide-and-seek game we're in.'

Matthew 7:7

'The person who trusts me will not only do what I'm doing but even greater things, because I, on my way to the Father, am giving you the same work to do that I've been doing. You can count on it. From now on, whatever you request along the lines of who I am and what I am doing, I'll do it. That's how the Father will be seen for who he is in the Son. I mean it. Whatever you request in this way, I'll do.'

John 14:12-14

'He was teaching in one of the meeting places on the Sabbath. There was a woman present, so twisted and bent over with arthritis that she couldn't even look up. She had been afflicted with this for eighteen years. When Jesus saw her, he called her over. "Woman, you're free!" He laid hands on her and suddenly she was standing straight and tall, giving glory to God.'

Luke 13:10-13

LET'S PRAY

❖ Pray for healing tonight, for each other and friends, relatives and church members who you know are unwell.

❖ Pray also for any situations or issues brought out of tonight's discussion time.

PRAYER JOURNAL SPACE

_____

_____

_____

_____

_____

_____

_____

_____

_____

_____

_____

_____

_____

_____

_____

_____

_____

_____

Reflections, learning points and ideas from this session...

BRING AND SHARE

A church get-together sees a crisis for Alice
and her newly married friend, Carly.

Bring and share lunches are terrifying at our church.

First, there's the panic over what to make. I go to a church that seems to be chock-a-block with bakers. Some of them even do it professionally. We don't just have rice salads; we have *risi e bisi* with a tofu twist. We don't just have fairy cakes; we have salted caramel cappuccino cupcakes with organic frosting topped with a home-roasted fair-trade Colombian coffee bean coated in hand-tempered Belgian chocolate.

And that's before we've even started talking about how it's going to be set up. My church is full of people who organise events for a living. *For a living!*

So, when it comes to the psychology of how the hall should be laid out, and the client-satisfaction-optimisation of the experience – well, let's just say it's covered.

There's not so much competition for the clearing up end of the event, though, despite us all being well experienced and qualified in the area of washing up and wiping down. This is where I usually find my home, with the other regular clearers, Phyllis Baynes, Deidre Hannon and Gladys Carmichael: me and the oldies. They joke that we should form a band, like Cliff and the Shadows: Alice and the Oldies.

This time, I've been braver than usual. I feel like God's telling me to step out a bit more. To stop hiding and get a bit more involved: I felt prompted to make a banana tray-bake. I've put it on a pink plate; a fat golden rectangle of sugary sponge, divided into squares. It had looked so tempting at home; the kitchen had filled with a warm, sweet fug and I'd felt domestic goddess status lay at last within my grasp.

And then I brought it to the buffet table.

The church hall looked lovely, with spotty bunting and lights hanging, and huge tissue paper pompoms hanging from the polystyrene tiled ceiling. It's a rather depressing post-war building, but they'd really cheered the place up. I approached the only remaining gap on the buffet table, between the brownies labelled (with miniature, handcrafted bunting suspended over them), 'Quadruple Choc Brownies' (how on earth can something be *quadruple* chocolate? I can't fathom it out) and 'Rich Caramel Truffle Millionaire's All-Butter Shortbread with Edible Gold-Leaf Topping Fit for a Queen.' I dropped my suddenly very plain-looking tray-bake between them and scarpered before any of the gathering congregation could know that it was mine.

I don't know who to sit with at church gatherings these days. Traditionally, Kat and Jo were my go-to pew-buddies, but now that they're both married, I find myself holding back a little. Three's a crowd, one way or another.

I've been a bridesmaid five times in the last two years. We all started internet dating and speed dating and Christian holidaying about four years ago, when we were twenty-eight and thirty was suddenly an actual real life age that we realised we were actually really going to be. And one by one, they've all paired off. Church these days reminds me of school discos, standing there alone at the edge, watching my friends getting asked up for the last dance, one by one.

I look around the room: my church family are milling around, deep in conversation in twos and threes. I don't see anyone I can latch onto, so I duck into the kitchen. There's always a friendly face in the kitchen, and I know just who'll be there.

Deidre Hannon is stout and strong. She's been a widow for forty-two years; her husband died just a year after they were married. She's got a son, whom she adores. Gladys Carmichael is tiny, bird-like, and twitchy. She writes poetry. Her husband, Roy, is still going strong, despite being deaf and walking with the aid of a frame these last months. Phyllis Baynes, tall and stern looking, has never been married. She may be eighty-seven, but she's still quite a rebel. It's always slightly nerve-wracking to sit next to her in church because if she disagrees with the preacher, she has no qualms about standing up and saying so. I suppose by the time you're eighty-seven, you're more experienced than most preachers in most spheres of life.

Phyllis won't be called spinster by anyone. Instead, she calls herself a 'spatula' - apparently when her nephew was little, he thought that was what single ladies were known as.

Hiding in the kitchen with my three oldies is nice. We make ourselves tea, and dip shortbread into it. Oldies don't count calories. Neither do they care about my love life: these three are pretty much the only people in church who never ask me if I have a young man *on the go*. It's like I can just relax. But I can't hang out with old women on a Friday night, can I? What good are these relationships to me when it comes to the long, slow twist of a lonely weekend? I'm thinking about this when the door explodes open and Carly bursts in.

I don't know what's wrong with Carly. Since she got married, all she does is cry. She and Josh have drama after drama after drama. Except Josh doesn't seem to have the dramas; it only seems to be Carly who's falling apart.

She stands in the middle of the small kitchen, eyes red and face blotchy.

'Everything alright, Carly?' Phyllis is the first to break the silence.

'I just - do you -' She looks around at us, blindly.

'Had another barny with Josh, have you?' Phyllis again.

'Don't worry, love, once you're through the first fifty years it gets much easier,' Gladys laughs and gives Carly's arm a squeeze.

I'm not sure how to respond to Carly's entrance. On the face of it, Carly has done the best out of all of them: her husband is a minister's son, hoping to train to go into the ministry himself. At 32, he has a PhD and is easily the best looking husband out of any of them. It's common knowledge that he's well respected amongst academics. Carly hit the jackpot there. God knows, I've prayed to have her problems!

'I'm so glad I never married,' Phyllis says, with all the tact of a wrecking ball hitting a doll's house. She picks up her mug and leaves the kitchen.

I feel torn. Carly is my friend, but surely Gladys is in a better position to comfort her than I am. What do I know? I don't have anything to offer in this situation.

'Here, there's not much a cup of tea can't help.' Gladys pours Carly a cup, adds milk and slips a shortbread onto the saucer before handing the medicine over. I wish I'd thought of that.

'Thanks.' Carly sniffs and half hugs Gladys as she takes the cup, spilling drink into the saucer. The spillage is enough to send her back to sobbing.

'Don't fret, that's what saucers are for, love.' Gladys reaches up her cardigan sleeve and pulls out a tissue. She checks it for lipstick, and then reaches out and dabs Carly's eyes with it. I watch with a twitch of envy, which Gladys must sense somehow, because she turns towards me, her eyes bright. 'I'd do the same for you, love,' is all she says. Carly looks at me too, then, in utter incomprehension.

She slurps at the tea, leaves the shortbread, rather ungratefully, I think, and puts the cup and saucer back on the side.

'Better?' Gladys asks. In response, Carly turns to me, opens her arms wide and wraps me in them, like she's binding me up with sticky tape. I hadn't seen it coming, but I hug back.

'I'm just being silly,' Carly says.

'What you need to remember is the good things,' Gladys cuts in. 'Don't tell yourself you have a perfect husband, tell yourself you have a good husband. Take the pressure off. He'll never be perfect, and neither will you. And that's fine.'

Deidre steps over to where Carly is still hanging on to me, and lays a tiny, slender hand on Carly's back. 'It's all building character to deal with the challenges of life that inevitably lie ahead, love,' she says gently.

'I never expected marriage to be so hard,' Carly says, her face buried in my shoulder. I look at Gladys and Deidre, expecting them to be rolling their eyes; instead they exchange knowing looks, the meaning of which I sense is steeped in history and experience. Gladys smiles at Deidre, who comes and stands by my side. The two women lay their arms around Carly and me, and the four of us hug, awkwardly, tensely on my part and Carly's. I sense an authority in the older women's arms that I long to feel for myself. Gladys speaks first, her voice calm, low, steady, certain.

'I'm talking to both of you,' she says. 'Married or single: relationships are hard work. That's that. They require a constant cycle of repentance, grace and mercy. Now, both of you, get back out there and fight for your relationships – for all of them.'

The two older women pull back from the hug. Carly steps back. My shoulder is soaked with her tears. Carly sees it and winces: I arrange my hair to cover the stain, and we smile at each other.

'Out you go,' Deidre says, smiling.

Carly opens the kitchen door, and I follow her back into the hall where the noise and hubbub is going on as if nothing has happened.

The church family have gone over the buffet table like locusts, and there are now just random slices of quiche and cake left, although the lettuce bowl is predictably still brim-full.

Instinctively, I go to see how my banana cake has fared. I brace myself to expect it to be untouched – after all, how could it compete with the fancy cakes surrounding it? Carly follows me and hears my exclamation.

'Everything alright?' she says.

'It's all gone!'

'Gone? Are you worried you've missed out – look, there's still plenty of cake. These ones are quadruple chocolate! And there's some millionaire's shortbread here, too.'

'My banana cake – it's all been eaten – and not as a last resort!'

Carly is looking at me with a strange expression; confusion, amusement... she can't work out what I'm on about. I smile and hug her again, much looser this time, happier; lighter inside and out.

'I'll have to make another one next time, now I know it's gone down so well.'

I pick up a quadruple chocolate brownie and bite into it.

'I always wonder how something can actually be quadruple chocolate,' Carly says. She's looking around the room.

'Go on, go and find him,' I say, giving her a peck on the cheek that leaves chocolate crumbs. I wipe them away with my thumb. 'Go and work it out.'

LET'S TALK

1. Did anything from this story strike a chord with you?

    _____

    _____

    _____

    _____

2. Intergenerational relationships play a key part in this story: does your church family contain a good mixture of ages and do you feel they mix well?

    _____

    _____

    _____

    _____

3. '...I'm talking to both of you,' she says. 'Married or single: relationships are hard work. That's that. They require a constant cycle of repentance, grace and mercy. Now, both of you, get back out there and fight for your relationships – for all of them.' This is the advice that Gladys Carmichael passes on to the younger women in this story. What do you think of her advice? What advice would you have given?

    _____

    _____

    _____

    _____

4. Do you have people in your church family who have years of experience and wisdom who you go to for advice? Do you feel the church values the knowledge and understanding of our older family members enough?

_____

_____

_____

_____

5. In this story, Alice is entirely lacking confidence about any offering she might bring to the church's lunch together. Do you feel you are able to contribute to your church family's life, and that your contribution is valued and valuable to the church? Why / why not?

_____

_____

_____

_____

6. How could you encourage someone else to let them know they are loved, valued and a special part of your church community? Is there a specific person that comes to mind who you could reach out to?

_____

_____

_____

_____

LET'S LISTEN

'Give your entire attention to what God is doing right now, and don't get worked up about what may or may not happen tomorrow. God will help you deal with whatever hard things come up whenever the time comes.'

Matthew 6:34

'Don't be afraid of missing out. You're my dearest friends! The Father wants to give you the very kingdom itself.'

Luke 12:32

'...Look at the ravens, free and unfettered, not tied down to a job description, carefree in the care of God. And you count far more. 'Has anyone by fussing before the mirror ever gotten taller by so much as an inch? If fussing can't even do that, why fuss at all? Walk into the fields and look at the wildflowers. They don't fuss with their appearance – but have you ever seen colour and design quite like it? The ten best-dressed men and women in the country look shabby alongside them. If God gives such attention to the wildflowers, most of them never even seen, don't you think he'll attend to you, take pride in you, do his best for you?'

Luke 12:24-28

'...Give a cool cup of water to someone who is thirsty, for instance. The smallest act of giving or receiving makes you a true apprentice. You won't lose out on a thing.'

Matthew 10:42

'...You see how every student well-trained in God's kingdom is like the owner of a general store who can put his hands on anything you need, old or new, exactly when you need it...'

Matthew 13:52

'You're blessed when you can show people how to cooperate instead of compete or fight. That's when you discover who you really are, and your place in God's family.'

Matthew 5:9

LET'S PRAY

❖ Pray for those who feel they have nothing to offer at church, that they will be valued and included, and that they'll feel able to actively contribute and their contribution will be welcomed.

❖ Pray for intergenerational links and relationships to grow and deepen within your church family.

❖ Pray that the church community will be a home for all – single, married, bereaved, young, old – that we really will be families where each member is loved and cared for.

PRAYER JOURNAL SPACE

_____

_____

_____

_____

_____

_____

_____

_____

_____

_____

_____

_____

_____

_____

_____

Reflections, learning points and ideas from this session...

AUTHOR NOTES

AUTHOR NOTES
STORY ONE

SAME TIME,
SAME PLACE

Themes covered by this story:

Prayer; miscommunication; rituals; isolation; missed opportunities; gossip; selfishness; causing and taking offence.

I feel so sorry for all the characters in this story! Except maybe Sammi, I feel quite frustrated by her; her heart's not in the people or the prayer. I could forgive her if I felt she was pouring all her energies into her children, but I don't see that being the case with Sammi. It would be better for her if she went to a prayer circle that didn't meet in her own home – but I'm not sure she'd bother.

The thing with Sammi is, she's doing what she sees as a 'duty.' In the same way that she's recently put someone from church up for a week on her sofa, it's all about 'the greater good and all that.' I'm sure she feels that, as hostess, she's 'doing her bit,' which makes her a rather hard-hearted character. She's busy for God, but what good is that doing her when the busyness is gone? She's an example of doing good things without love, which feels very empty to me. I feel so cross with her at the end for shutting that door on Franklin!

And why didn't Franklin tell them about his visit to the doctor? He is seriously ill, you know: the prayer group will find out about it in a few weeks' time – although, not through him during a prayer session, I'm sorry to say. They'll hear about it on the church gossip grapevine, and then they'll feel too awkward to mention it until he brings it up. Oh dear, poor, lonely Franklin! I feel terrible for him – he needs to be more forthcoming, but in this environment, he's never going to open up. He really needs to join a different group.

My heart goes out to Marjorie, too. Yes, she's a bit of a nit picking, judgmental busy body, but in my imagination, she lives on beyond the story, as do all the characters in this book. Marjorie's health is about to decline rapidly, and this group will be no support to her whatsoever. In fact, they'll withdraw. Franklin won't be in good health himself, and Sammi doesn't care for Marjorie. Gloria will visit her occasionally, but she and Marjorie don't really connect, besides which, I see Gloria moving away in the not-too-distant future: she meets someone online, and drops everything to go and be where he is, at the other end of the country.

This story started out as a drawing. I sketched the prayer group, sitting in Sammi's lounge, viewed from above. The characters very quickly got out of their chairs and strolled around in my mind, and showed me just how this group was not working for them.

Prayer can be a very difficult thing to do as a group; it's so easy to get distracted into chat and catching up. It's so easy for gossip to be slipped in as a prayer request!

Have you ever had the experience of sitting in your small group, having had a great evening together, and then you come to the time of prayer before you all depart – because often prayer is used as punctuation, a sort of closing bracket to the evening, isn't it? And the person leading that session says 'Let's move into a time of prayer,' or something similar, in a voice that isn't quite their own, and is nothing like any voices used by anyone in the previous hour. Everybody tenses slightly, sits straighter, draws their legs in, and prepares to *Pray*.

At times in my life I've been in groups where we've gone round the circle, with each person stating their prayer request. We may have spent our small group evening discussing something that feels quite detached to everyday life, and then, because of a prayer request, we discover that someone in the group is about to go into hospital the next day for a serious operation – and we only have five minutes to pray about it! The people following on from this needy soul in the circle hastily readjust their priorities and decide that prayer for their heavy workload or nasty boss or stroppy toddler or slow house sale etc etc really don't matter that much anymore, and give that classic response when asked 'What can we pray for you?': 'Nothing thanks, I'm fine.'

Then there's that waiting at the end, when the last prayer has been said, only no-one knows it was the last prayer until two people shuffle their feet and sniff simultaneously. Slowly, cautiously, the rest of the group shuffle and sniff and start to think about where their coats and car keys are, and the evening is over.

It's so difficult, isn't it?! I don't have any answers – I might have written a very different book if I did. But perhaps through an open, honest discussion about the way we pray in groups, your group will find a better way forward.

When we discussed this in our group, it was very releasing. Prayer within our group is changing slowly as a result of having read this story, but the main difference is that we're all approaching it with more humour and a newly shared awareness of just how peculiar we Christians can be when we get together!

AUTHOR NOTES
STORY TWO

DOUBLE FIGURES

Themes covered by this story:

Family cultures; language; personal baggage; double standards; inconsistency; secular and sacred divide; parenting; growing up.

W hen I tested this story out on my small group, it led to a fascinating conversation about our family cultures growing up. Externally, we all appeared quite similar in a tick-box survey kind of way. What we discovered was that our upbringings were vastly different, from class to religion to family structure. It was a night of surprises, which led to much greater understanding of each other and a new appreciation for each other's experiences.

This story is heavily influenced by my own experience as a parent of small children, and by my experiences growing up in a vicarage. I remember as a child thinking all adults were Christians, and undergoing a long and confusing re-think when it dawned on me that this was not the case at all.

I also remember trying to fathom out whether my family didn't swear because we were Christians, or because we were middle class. It's a very hard distinction to make for a child (maybe for an adult, too), because a lot of Christian living – kindness, thoughtfulness, putting others first, loving others and so on – can be seen as plain old good manners that enable a smooth running, pleasant society. For example, when I was a child at home, we weren't allowed to say 'crap' – that was a Very Bad Word. But saying 'crap' is quite disconnected from accepting Jesus as my

Lord and Saviour, isn't it? I'm saying this, but I'm not entirely sure that I know the answer! I still carry all the hazy confusion of my own upbringing.

In all family cultures, there's a mix of the social conventions of the time, the conventions your parents grew up with and brought from their own homes, and all sorts of other misty politic – dynamics, necessities, environment – the variables are endless.

I find it so hard to be consistent, and I so admire others who speak openly and freely when they describe their faith experiences to non-believers. I'm of the nervous toe-tapping, awkward mumbling school of verbal faith sharing – a very short Christian indeed.

AUTHOR NOTES
STORY THREE

YOURS
FAITHFULLY

Themes covered by this story:

*Prejudice; loneliness; sadness;
emotional intelligence; spiritual maturity;
feeling on the fringes of church; complaining; self-awareness.*

I've mentioned before that I grew up in a vicarage, and my experience is that there are plenty of Eva Bishops out there! My dear Dad really had the patience of a saint with everyone, and gave his love indiscriminately – occasionally to my utter shock as a child – *How could Dad give so much time to that nasty old whatsit...?!*

I think he must have done it because he discerned the subtext of people's lives, the real issues going on between the lines. There's always a reason behind a person's behaviour, the outer expression merely pointing to the inner emotion or motivation. In screenwriting, the saying goes 'action is character' – that is, you show who a person is by what they do. It's true in all of life.

Easy as it is to condemn Eva Bishop as a judgemental busybody, if we're really, painfully, embarrassingly honest, we can all tend to think the exact same way she does.

We all have a little inner Eva Bishop, whispering critical phrases and cutting us off from those around us.

This is the heart of what I hope to get to with this story. If we condemn Eva outright, we do just as she does.

AUTHOR NOTES
STORY FOUR

BACK IN THE DAYS WHEN THE PICTURES CAME

Themes covered by this story:

Hearing from God; jealousy; judgementalism; insecurity in our identity; repentance; honesty; accountability; status; pride; ego.

Pride takes centre stage in this story. It's also about how you can have seasons when God speaks to you loads, and then suddenly it's as if the line's gone dead. In Sharon's case, she's been fostering a misplaced pride and sense of identity over her regular words for the church, so that when someone else hears from God and she doesn't, she feels it as a very personal affront.

'Her next door neighbours heard about her through friends of theirs and came to see for themselves.' This line implies a lack of Monday to Saturday witness, and reinforces the idea that church has become a performance for Sharon, with Sundays as her focus. After all, why did her neighbours have to hear about her even going to church through friends? Something's amiss here.

'She's been a Jehovah's Witness or a Mormon or something like that (Sharon could never remember which)...' Again, this sentence, those brackets, are pointing towards Sharon's level – or lack of – engagement with others. She has become the object of her own focus, to the exclusion of others. As the saying goes, 'When a man gets wrapped up in himself, he makes a pretty small parcel.'

There are signs that Sharon's developed rather a consumer attitude to church – 'The worship just wasn't moving her lately...' It's a shocking way to approach a service, but I've been guilty of feeling like that sometimes: have you?

This misplaced focus is skewing everything else in Sharon's perspective; she's become cynical and judgmental. When she describes Lola as the pastor's 'new favourite,' we see how complex and confused her thinking is: she's approaching things with herself, not Christ, as centre-stage. And, as she increasingly brushes Jonathan's attempts at affection and support away, we see how the cynicism is infecting her relationship with him.

When she starts interpreting Lola's behaviour as 'less nervy, more... cocky,' Sharon's really lost it. This description has nothing to do with Lola's behaviour and says everything about Sharon's state of heart. In this hateful state, can she expect to hear a word from God to encourage the church? When she views Lola as pausing 'for laughter,' the implication is that Sharon views the congregation as an audience, and the person on the platform as some sort of entertainer.

However, I feel there is hope for Sharon. When she sinks to her knees at the end of the story, she's been convicted very deeply. We leave her in a truly agonising place of self-realisation. In my mind, she stays there and weeps for some time, convicted, repenting, feeling increasingly humbled. I then see her standing up and confessing her resentment to Jonathan, and then to Lola herself – with the pastor's help. She makes peace, and she grows through the experience. And on the next Alpha course, she signs up to stack the chairs at the end of the evening!

Pride is the enemy we must be wary of. It can seep in whether you're on the stage or stacking the chairs in church, and it ruins our relationship with Christ and with those around us. We can even feel pride in being 'humble' enough to confess our pride! Following Christ certainly makes life interesting, doesn't it?! It calls us to account, to scratch the surface and to confront and confess what lies beneath.

AUTHOR NOTES
STORY FIVE

WINNING

Themes covered by this story:

Competitiveness; comparing ourselves; parenting; vanity; pride; selfishness; motivation; Holy Spirit convicting; self-deception.

Over the years, I've written articles for a variety of Christian NGOs about people doing amazing work on their behalf, as well as having friends and church family who've gone overseas to join ministries and plant churches. Inevitably, when others make these courageous decisions, it causes us to pause and reflect on our own lives, and maybe question ourselves: why aren't I doing that?

I believe God's got a different plan for each of us, and I'm sure there's plenty of mission opportunity for you right where you are at this moment, wherever in the world that may be. But I thought it would be fun to explore the reactions of a couple who are completely open with each other, oblivious to their shocking attitudes and not at all self-conscious about expressing them. Karen and Morris aren't unique - they're just uncensored!

'Confusion gave way to relief, and then guilt...'

Morris is introduced as a mixed up bundle of emotions. In church, as everywhere else, we are emotional human beings, and we do well to remember how temporary and fleeting emotional experience is. Morris and Karen's reaction is human and understandable - it's what they do with it that takes them to new depths.

The overall tone of this story is very tongue in cheek, especially with lines like:

'No one will think we're roughing it enough if we tell them we're going to Australia...'

And:

'What about China?'

'I don't want to actually *endanger* our children's lives simply for the sake of proving a point.'

And:

'...Bangladesh – well, is there really any help for Bangladesh? With all that flooding? Would we be wasting our time?'

However, even within these outrageous lines of dialogue, I recognise my own weak tendencies and temptations. There's a Sara Groves song called 'This Journey Is My Own,' in which she talks about doubting our own motivation for following Christ, concerned more about the impression we're making on the people around us. Living as a Christian can lead to a very complex inner life, can't it?! We constantly fight the sin of pride, so that even when we are doing good, we are keeping a check on whom we are doing the good for. It's exhausting!

Perhaps the tragedy of this tale is that, in their thinking about their children, we do see something of Morris and Karen's hearts:

'All those bedtime prayers, all those bible studies... the repetition, the tedium, the constant drumming it all in... what's it all been for, Karen?'

That's a really sad sentence, isn't it? Morris and Karen are looking to their children to enhance their own standing in front of others. It's so tempting to do this as a parent! It's so wonderful when your kids do something amazing in church and everyone sees it and celebrates it... and it's so crushing when your kids do something less than amazing and everyone sees that!

There's no doubt that Morris and Karen are placing unrealistic hopes and pressures upon their offspring, but the process of writing this story also made me think of the number of biblical parents who were perhaps embarrassed by their children – right from Adam and Eve: children are no guarantee of glory or satisfaction in life.

Karen makes herself feel better by comparing her kids with the others in church:

'I agree, there's loads of awful kids at church.'

Her heart is revealed in this sentence: she's busy looking left and right, and not bothering to look up.

When the couple hit on the idea of calling their holiday a 'family team building' exercise they well and truly lose themselves to pride. How tempting it is to put a 'holy' spin on our simple, maybe even selfish, intentions! How attractive it is to dress things up, rather than simply admit we are just enjoying life without any further aim than enjoyment.

The feeling in Karen's belly that occurs twice in this story is a prompting from the Holy Spirit. I'm not sure if Karen will ever acknowledge it – as characters, Karen and Morris are horribly lost in a web of spin. It will take a 'Damascus Road' experience to bring them to their senses and pull them from their self-delusional state. I worry a bit for their children.

AUTHOR NOTES
STORY SIX

FACE
PAINTING

Themes covered by this story:

*Honesty; identity; work; witness; outreach;
finding rest in surprising places;
preconceptions and prejudice;
being your true self in church.*

This was one of the first stories I wrote, and it went through many drafts and changes before it settled into the shape it's in here. I didn't want to be overly simplistic and I didn't want a clear cut goody/ baddy scenario between Willow and David.

These characters were inspired by a response I received over twenty years ago to an article I'd written for the Church of England Newspaper.

My article was about how married people were just as apt in church to experience loneliness as single people were. At that time, I'd been writing for a few years about how tough it was to be single in church – and then I got married, and discovered I'd been wrong about single people having the monopoly on feeling isolated within their congregations.

I received a letter from a lady who'd read the article. She was elderly, her husband was the organist in their church – and he was a very gifted organist, admired by all in the congregation. But while he attracted praise and attention, his wife felt trapped in the background, unnoticed and uncared for. Each week she sat alone at the back of the side aisle, listening to him play, and feeling thoroughly cut off from everybody else in her congregation.

This woman's expression of loneliness affected me deeply – and still does. I expect she will rise again in other stories and forms, because her words were so full of feeling and sadness. I wanted to explore loneliness in church, and it seemed to me more poignant if explored through characters that everybody thinks of as central and 'established' in a congregation.

In this story, face painting is used as a metaphor for covering our true faces to appear a certain way. Just as the children in Willow's queue all choose Spiderman, so we can all choose a particular look in the belief that it will be acceptable, make us happier, and turn us into someone else, at least until we wipe it off.

I've painted Willow as someone who has not been voicing her opinions – when she talks about how face painting whilst keeping an eye on her own children is proving as impossible as she'd expected, there's a hint as to part of the cause of her loneliness: she's not expressing herself to others. I'm a sort of introverted extrovert, if that makes any sort of sense. My inner thought life can absorb me utterly – and yet I can feel isolated if I lock myself inside my own head and then grieve others' apparent lack of understanding of me – as if I expect them to read my mind!

'He must have walked past her again without seeing her...'

How often we miss the needs of those closest and dearest to us, because we are wrapped up in our own busyness! We may be busy doing good stuff – but the challenge is to remain alert to those around us, not to lose ourselves in the practical task we're accomplishing, but to remain conscious of the bigger picture. Easier said than done.

Eleanor is obviously used symbolically here, too. Just as Jesus was an outsider who brought freedom and release from religious oppression in his day, so Eleanor comes and rescues Willow, offering practical care, rest and comfort. When Eleanor tucks the children under her arms like chicks, it's a clear reference to the refuge offered in Matthew 23:38: '...How often I've ached to embrace your children, the way a hen gathers her chicks under her wings...'

Jesus understands how 'doing' church is not the same as 'being' church.

AUTHOR NOTES
STORY SEVEN

FAMILIAR
STRANGERS

Themes covered by this story:

'Church-hopping'; friendship; roots;
relationships within church; patterns of behaviour;
avoidance; isolation; self-exclusion.

I'm rather fond of Travis. He's looking for family and security, but family can be a rather uncomfortable place at times, and this doesn't fit with his wish-list.

I would be tempted to move on, just as Travis does. I often feel I'd happily go to a different church every Sunday – that way, I'd get to enjoy lots of different styles of preaching and singing, and be on those wonderfully friendly terms that visitors get welcomed with in most churches! It's smiles all round and no expectations whatsoever when you're not regular, isn't it?

Of course, church isn't the only place like this. But it's church that I'm exploring in these stories, and Travis's experience is probably not that unusual.

He's been unlucky to a degree – a relationship break up with a minister's daughter is to my mind a very understandable reason for moving on from a place. It's interesting though, how many Christians are moving around from one church to another; I have a feeling they get slightly frowned upon, and through the character of Travis I wanted to explore the reasons why someone might move churches. The experiences he has are all very 'human', but is there a spiritual element underlying them?

I once heard that you need seven friends to hold you to a church – I'm not sure if that's right, but I'm certain that friendship is hugely important within church. In an earlier version I wrote of this story, Travis was working for the railways, and he'd found a circle of friends there who had become his family. It didn't quite work in that version, I wanted more to confront Travis with the detritus of his movements, and the back pew at a wedding was a better place to explore that.

When people leave a church, it is painful for those left behind. They wonder why, but most people are too polite to ask the question, so we form our own opinions and jump to the wrong conclusions, and the hurt settles in. Meanwhile, the person who left rarely gets pursued or even asked why they aren't attending any more – and so has no opportunity to defend or explain their decision.

Perhaps it's a 'British' thing on both sides of the experience; all about reserve and not wishing to cause discomfort or embarrassment.

I've been in small groups, too, where members have left to join other groups – that's tough, isn't it? It's tricky for those who leave, and it's hard on those who are left. Is it a case of simply 'blooming where you're planted,' or should you go and seek alternative soil sometimes?

I hope Travis continues in his relationship with Jesus. I'm honestly not sure what way it'll go for him. Do you think he'll ever settle somewhere? With no blood-relations, he's rather rootless, I fear. I hope he finds a place where he feels accepted and where he gets involved in contributing.

Playing a part *in* church is crucial to *feeling* a part *of* church. Until you get involved, it can be easy to consume and walk away. Travis has talents; what he needs is for them to be picked up on by a church leader of some sort, so that he can start giving of himself to the family community. This story reminds me to look out for those on the fringes, and to invite them to use their talents and become practically knitted into the family God has for them.

AUTHOR NOTES
STORY EIGHT

HOUSE GROUP LEADER
ON THE EDGE

Themes covered by this story:

*Leadership; group membership; honesty;
respect; busyness; resentment; anger; losing your temper; pride
before a fall.*

This story felt very daring to write! The tricky thing with fiction is that friends who read your stories presume that you are writing about your own experience, and consequently try to piece the elements together to work out 'who's who' within the story from the real world. It's an awful experience, and could stop me writing altogether if I gave in to the feelings of vulnerability and misconception it brings up. Years ago I wrote a story about a parent getting sucked into the madness of a toddler tantrum, which led to a friend deciding I must have once taken a wee in my own back garden when my daughter was a toddler. The more I protest, the more she can picture me doing it.

In that spirit, let me state for the record that I have never been tempted to - crumble a Rich Tea biscuit over anyone's head.

That said, I have been involved in leading small groups where members are dreadful at replying to any communications; I have also been a member of a small group and been myself guilty of failing to reply to the leader's communications. I think texting may be partly to blame: it's so easy to think 'I'll reply later,' and then to forget. In the '90s when I was co-leading a group, none of us had mobile phones yet, so we had a programme that we put together at the beginning of the term, and if people came, they came. We were in a very good small group at the time,

174

where there was quite a bit of communication between our meetings, so we generally knew what was going on with people and whether to expect them on the Thursday evening.

Having facilitated several small groups now, and attended many, many church small group leaders' meetings, I think the administration side of a small group can be a real turn off for prospective leaders. I've seen small group leaders in tears over the lack of response they regularly receive from people who've been in their group for years, who know just how busy they are and how hard it is for them to run the small group on top of all their other commitments. It feels dreadfully disrespectful to these hard working people whose intention and aim is so good and so important to a healthy church.

On the other hand, I didn't want to paint Peter as some sort of saint: he's a human being, and he gets things wrong, too.

I hope he calls his small group together for an extraordinary meeting, comes clean with them about the stress he's under and the difficulty he's experienced in communicating with them, and then, perhaps, I think dear old Peter should maybe take a break from leading for a while. He doesn't have much fun in his life, does he? It's all work and duty, and that's not doing him any good.

AUTHOR NOTES
STORY NINE

A FAMILY
CRISIS

Themes covered by this story:

*Fear; fight or flight; life experience and baggage;
feeling safe; small group culture; honesty; courage; change;
welcoming new members.*

'I used to love home group. They were six of the nicest people I knew.'
For Edith, home group is a safe place. One of the things I wanted to explore here is how we can easily surround ourselves with lovely Christian friends who are just like us, and how this makes us feel 'safe.'

Perhaps home groups *should* be like this – I haven't written this story with any right or wrong answer in mind.

I feel great empathy and sadness for Edith Pinn. In the fight or flight battle, she is definitely 'flight', and yet she had an opportunity here – in this 'safe place' - to work through a fear with friends who would pray for her. I believe that, had she stayed in the group, she would have found release from the frightening experience she had as a child in that bird cage, an experience which is holding her captive.

But, of course, that's easier said than done. When one is afraid, one's actions are all about survival, and self-preservation.

Edith has given up praying about her fear – and yet, could it be that Tony Partridge is the answer to her prayer? That God brought him to Edith's group for a reason?

May's words are unhelpful; people who don't share a fear can often make those who genuinely feel afraid feel belittled and embarrassed on top of their fear.

176

Edith would accuse Tony of being her enemy, but he's not - in fact, he's her potential hero in this scenario. There are several 'crimes' in this story: firstly, the Baxters, and Edith's parents, who both let Edith down very badly in her youth by locking her in that cage and then making her feel ashamed of feeling afraid and abandoned; secondly, May's thoughtless quick and easy approach to solving Edith's problems, which reiterates the social embarrassment for Edith and takes her back to that place of shame with all its associated desires to run away; thirdly, Edith is her own worst enemy (as we all so often are). In failing to be honest about her fear and to subsequently allow others to help her walk gently through it, and to trust that God is bigger than any fear she feels, she is cheating herself out of her Christian birth-right of courage in her heavenly father's name.

I say all these things with the awareness that I myself have battled with many, many fears and phobias over the years - and I have failed at overcoming so many of them. I know that, were I Edith, I may well run as she does. I want to be someone who would speak honestly to my home group, without fear of rejection or embarrassment, and who would take steps, trusting the promises of God, and prove his word true.

Something I wanted to include within this story is the way that Edith's group, although safe and comfortable, clearly has very little vulnerability or accountability within it. In fact, vulnerability and accountability are the opposite of safe and comfortable! I know that the times I've grown most have been when I've been accountable and vulnerable with people - but this can be impossible in a large group. Accountability seems to work best for me in a one-to-one relationship - how do you find it? Is it something you're actively encouraging within your group? If so, how's it going? If not, do you feel there's space for it, and how could it work?

I know from experience that it's entirely possible to go to a home group evening and reveal nothing of what's really going on in your life to the others there - and I also know the empty, pointless frustration caused by this experience.

'...and we all knew that the church was growing...'

This is also a story about change. Small groups can be like lifeboats in a large church - but of course, change is an inevitable part of life, and can be extremely unsettling and frightening for people. There is so much rapid change going on all around us in this age, and when it hits the church, it can feel like your anchor has been lifted and left hanging in open seas - I guess this is the danger of putting your hope in church, rather than in Christ, who holds firm and of course, is the true anchor that we can count on: our hope and faith is not in the sand the anchor sinks into, or the waters through which is passes, nor in the boat it tethers, however large and impressive the boat may be.

'I didn't know anything about Tony. I wasn't sure he'd fit in.'

This idea was me thinking about how we like people to be explainable and understandable – to fit our idea of the right mould. When we meet people who don't sit neatly with everyone else we know, be it due to their class or appearance, ideology or approach to life, we can really struggle to accept them into our circles. Christ is utterly inclusive – the most inclusive being that ever lived and walked the earth – and yet, church can sometimes feel nothing like this. And I speak as a very short Christian here, without any accusation of others - I am a part of the very church I speak of, and guilty of prejudging and bias and excluding, to my shame. It's the same with all these stories – I feel, experience and perpetrate the very emotions I explore; it's the purpose of this fiction, so I hope you will never feel when reading that I am pointing any fingers at anyone – all fingers are welcome to point in my direction!

When it comes to counselling Edith, May is not exactly the Queen of Tact and Diplomacy:

'There you go – all sorted!'

May's words at first glance demonstrate an over-simplistic view of the complicated nature of Edith's phobia – or do they? If Edith did give her fear to God and actually let go, perhaps it *would* be 'all sorted.' At times we can hold on to fears - somehow we feel safer with the 'devil we know'. But how can God take our fears while we cling to them?

However, it is the person who experiences the fear who needs reach this point of trust and surrender. Edith's fears are not just of birds, but also of others' opinions of her. When she feels anxious about May's opinion, she feels hatred towards her – a defensive response.

We need to have empathy and understanding for the Ediths amongst us – this story may apply in different ways for each member of your group. We all face fears and anxieties as we go through life, and we have the most extraordinary resource in God to help us through those fears – the key is perhaps not to get in his way, but to look for opportunities to be his instrument of love and service to one another, to build one another up and applaud as we watch one another grow.

AUTHOR NOTES
STORY TEN

DEGREES OF SEPARATION

Themes covered by this story:

Wrong assumptions; jumping to conclusions; friendship; judging others; parenting; children; family; hospitality; risk; swearing.

I have great fondness for both Tish and Bridget: I feel their pain! My children are still fairly young, and over the years they've brought me tremendous amounts of embarrassment in church by making a big deal out of strange smells and refusing to conform or cooperate just at the moments I'd really like them to.

Parenthood is tough. No surprises there. But doesn't it become all the more complicated in church, when we're trying to conform to certain modes of what we perceive as acceptable behaviour? Sometimes, taking a small child to church can be very stressful. I say sometimes, but my experience was more 'weekly' than sometimes! (I must add, the stress was mostly self-induced).

We can be our own harshest critics, and see disapproval where none is intended when it comes to our children. We feel things so personally, because our hearts are so wrapped around them.

It's also so easy to see something happening and jump to the wrong conclusion the way that Bridget does when she sees Tish breastfeeding Toby in the car. At some point in their relationship, they'll discover that they both had problems with this and Bridget will have to reassess the assumptions she so wrongly made about Tish before she knew her. This kind of mistake is so easy to make in church, and yet it has a power to divide us; we really need to guard against making decisions based on first impressions, which are weighed down often by our own baggage and prejudice.

It's only when Tish takes a risk and invites Bridget into her home and Bridget likewise takes a risk and accepts the invitation that these women can begin to move past their misconceptions about each other and find the connections that will lead them to genuine friendship. The invitation and the acceptance both require vulnerability – a willingness to show who they are outside of the church environment, where behaviour and reactions can be monitored, channelled and controlled. It's scary to be open in this way with others, but it changes relationships entirely when we get together over a meal – as Jesus well knew.

I love Tish and Bridget, they've got bags in common – and I know that they're going to become very good friends. As their kids get older, they'll still meet for meals. Jake will go to university, Seth will take on a local apprenticeship. Ellie will get through her strops, Mia will be an easy teen, having got lots out of her system very early on(!) Toby will grow up worshipping Jake and Seth, and the kids will grow to be more like cousins – right up until the moment when, aged twenty-one, Jake and Ellie finally give in to the feelings that have been growing over the years, and kiss one another tenderly under the boughs of the apple tree that grows in her mum's garden...

Over the years, Tish and Bridget will never cease to roar with laughter whenever the 'shit on the rug' is mentioned. The friendship these women share is a gift from God, and will continue to bless them and comfort them their whole lives long.

AUTHOR NOTES
STORY ELEVEN

GRAHAM STOOD
BY THE COT

Themes covered by this story:

*Healing; preaching; life experience;
disappointment with God; prayer; hope; despair; grace;
righteousness before God; doubt; confusion.*

Healing: now there's a nice, light subject for a story...!

I've had lots of experience of praying for healing and nothing happening. I prayed – as many did – for my father, who loved God more than anyone else I've ever known, and who was suffering from a long-term degenerative disease. His mind was sharp, his heart still longing to do God's will, but his body had completely failed him, and kept him bed-bound. He wasn't healed. He used to say, 'God is certainly teaching me something through this, but I cannot for the life of me think what it is yet.' It would have been to God's great glory to have raised him up onto his feet – so why didn't it happen? I guess I'll have to wait for that answer, because I can't fathom it out.

I know so many wonderful Christians who've died too young, leaving children and partners and parents to carry the hidden scars of loss. It's horrible! And I confess, it's incomprehensible to me. I'm not the first to ask why bad things happen to good people, and I certainly won't be the last.

I've also has just enough experience of healing prayers being answered positively – both my own and other people's - to drive me to keep hoping and trying. But I can't claim to see any patterns or reasons for the healing either way, and so healing remains a murky area to me, and the risk and fears associated with offering it remain.

This story will hopefully help you to discuss the possibility of miracles, and how you all feel about their lack of regularity or predictability. I often think of how Peter's shadow would heal people that he passed, and wonder at how this state of affairs came to be – it's an idea put by Graham, when he says '*I know God's actions are not about my performance, and that it's all about grace, I know that in my head, but right now, at this moment, I can't help but wonder...*' What does your group *really* think?

There's a moment of false hope, when the test readings come back positive and Graham feels his prayer has been answered. I've known that to happen, and when it does, my temptation is to explain away God's apparent failure to answer my prayers with rationales like 'It's not a 'no,' it's a 'not yet',' or 'God's answer will come through the medical staff and the next blood transfusion...'

I've heard speakers talk about how, in the West, because we have such good medical provision, we tend to have less dependence on God – and I can see how this is true. Often when I've been with others praying for healing, we fall between two camps of prayer. We start out praying for the healing to happen right now in Jesus' name, and then, as we wait and watch and nothing seems to be happening, the prayers change tack: 'If it doesn't happen at this moment, we pray for good doctors and medical staff so that X gets the help they need...'

It would be so different if healing was guaranteed to work like magic every time we asked for it – and yet, this seems to be just how it was for Peter and his shadow.

I decided to give this story a church elder as its central character and to make the nurse a Christian too, to enable a full exploration of these views on healing – the supernatural and the natural. Graham's first instinct is prayer followed by an expectation of success, while the Matron's attitude is that 'In my experience, miracles take a while.' They're all good people trying to follow Christ in their own lives – and for some reason on this day, God has apparently not answered their prayers for healing. The object of that healing is an innocent child, knitted together by God, and loved by him – again, this adds to the confusion: why not heal her?

I wrote this story in a supermarket café, and the final scene with the three women and the disabled children was going on as I wrote.

Use this story to help you get deep into your shared experiences and ideas around healing. Encourage people to voice doubts freely, to question God boldly; it's an area some people may well feel angry towards God about because they might feel they've been ignored, missed out or let down by him.

AUTHOR NOTES
STORY TWELVE

BRING AND
SHARE

Themes covered by this story:

*Singleness; marriage; widowhood; identity; church family;
acceptance; guidance; discipleship; perfectionism;
loneliness; belonging.*

When I was single, I often felt lonely in church, and as if my contribution was much less than that of the more 'established,' and 'grown up' people around me. Then I got married and discovered I still felt exactly the same! Ha!

That's one of the issues at the heart of Bring and Share. The story's written in the first person, because it's all about the narrator's skewed perspective; she thinks her cake is not so worthy as other peoples, and she thinks she has nothing to offer a friend in a crisis: neither feeling is true.

I have a tremendous respect for older members of the church - they have such wisdom and experience that they can share. I wish they'd speak out more often, and that they had a greater voice. By the time you get to 70, you've seen and done so many things, and, if you've been walking through those years with God, you'll have accumulated such wisdom and insight. Not that I wish to put older people on a pedestal here - Phyllis is lovely but somewhat lacking in compassion. But Gladys and Deirdre speak the truth in love to Carly and our narrator, and the result is clear direction, and a change of heart.

Something else in this story, which I only really touch on here through the character of Carly, is how difficult life for newly-weds can be. My memories of our first year of marriage are generally stormy. It took a lot to get used to living with someone else all the time, and I'm not sure how well the church prepares people for this reality. Marriage can often be held up as a rather idealised state, which leads to single people thinking that this is the thing they should be praying for and dreaming of. I'm pleased that, although others think Carly a bit of a mess and a drama queen, she's at least seeking some help publicly – I never dared to share my difficulties at settling into married life with others in such a public way, as I had this misconception that we were the only ones finding it hard to get used to and therefore the problem was us. It's easy to look back now, in my middle age, and to see that it was normal to have some hiccups at the start, but Carly doesn't have this luxury of hindsight just yet.

So it's really a story about some of the different stages of life that people go through – singleness, marriage and widowhood – and looking at how we have something to offer our church family, and indeed the world, at every step of our journey.

I hope this story's narrator retains that feeling of having contributed something of value to her church's feast, and I hope she also realises that marriage is not the holy grail of happiness. Most of all, I want her to feel very much at home within her church family; valued as she is, celebrated for her God-given talents and engaged in meaningful relationships that direct her towards Christ and his love for her.

NOTES

NOTES

ABOUT THE AUTHOR

Liz Jennings grew up in a South London vicarage in the 1970s, the youngest of three children. Their home was a lively one, with a constant flow of interesting characters, from the homeless men she and her brothers would make sandwiches for after school to the various church workers who lodged with them, the church family who peopled the endless meetings in the front room and the occasional visiting Ugandan bishop. At sixteen, she moved with her parents to the Midlands, returning to London two years later to study for an English and Theology degree. She has spent her working life writing whenever possible, and trying other random jobs in between, from guiding people around a Roman museum to invigilating GCSEs in a never ending habit of curiosity. She has written features and fiction for a variety of Christian and secular publications, from Tearfund to Take A Break. In recent years, she has become involved in setting up and running writing groups with and for people with a diagnosis of dementia. She met her husband, Mark, while temping in Clapham. They have two children, Maisie and Reuben, and live in Kent.

Lightning Source UK Ltd.
Milton Keynes UK
UKOW01f2141241017
311572UK00007B/254/P